What readers are saying about this book:

"I love irony, and it works particularly well here. Nice job."

"This is what makes the book so fun to read. Nice storytelling."

"Great job with these press conferences and their spin."

"This is too good. Love it!"

"Just clever writing."

"This is great! Laughed out loud."

"I laughed out loud, thought the parody was spot on, and enjoyed the satire."

"Oh, this cracked me up! Classic. Love it. Well done."

"You use similes so wisely—and they're so apropos to the story too."

ZOMBIE TURKEYS

Andy Zach

Zombie Turkeys: How an Unknown Blogger
Fought Unkillable Turkeys

Copyright © 2016 by Andy Zach
First Edition, 2016

Cover Illustration and jacket design: Sean Patrick Flanagan
Edited by: Dori Harrell
Formatting by Rik: Wild Seas Formatting
(http://www.WildSeasFormatting.com)
Published by: Jule Inc.

PO Box 10705
Peoria, Illinois 61612
zombieturkeys.com

ISBN: 978-1-5394667-5-8

To the love of my life, my wife

Acknowledgments

Although I have already dedicated this book to my wife, Julie, I want to acknowledge her first, for encouraging me to keep at it through the months of writing and editing it required. Since I'm going in time order, other people who have encouraged me include my sister, Bonnie Green; my friend Jerry Moehn; and my children, Tori, Olivia, Raymond, and daughter-in-law Jacqueline. The children were initial readers who gave invaluable feedback, making the book much better. Tori also worked hard on the web promotion of the book.
I must also mention my diligent editor, Dori Harrell. How helpful was she? I plan to use her for all the books in the *Zombie Turkey* series.

Sean Patrick Flanagan executed the book cover illustration with his normal panache. Thank you, Sean.

Foreword

Wow. I doubt I could have written this story about Lisa and me better than Andy did. Sure, I can blog and write newspaper copy, but actually writing a book?

It was kind of fun, being the one interviewed this time, rather than interviewing. Some of Andy's questions were really penetrating, getting into what I thought and felt at different stages in the story. I hadn't really analyzed them before. He brought things out of me I didn't know I had in me.

You probably already know that Dr. Andy Zach is the foremost paranormal animal expert. His seminal paper "Methods of Revivification for Various Species of the Kingdom Animalia" has been used by the Turkey Institute and every paranormal animal research lab in the country.

In addition to being a genius, Andy is very modest. No one would ever know he has a PhD in paranormal animal physiology. Fortunately, I'm a professional reporter and can find out this kind of obscure information. So when he approached me to turn our reporting into a book, I researched Andy Zach to the nth degree. Being highly impressed by his PhD paper, what I could understand of it, I agreed to let him write our story. I, of course, retained editorial control—or rather, Lisa Kambacher, my editor, did.

Reading his first draft, I was amazed how matter of factly, but accurately, he described our incredible experiences. Were I not there, I would have thought I was the hero. I encouraged him to tone down his descriptions. Very reluctantly, Andy agreed.

So if anyone wants to criticize Andy's account as being too bland or boring, put all the blame on me. I am, after all, bland and boring.

—Sam Melvin, Investigative Reporter for the *Midley Beacon*
Famous Zombie Turkey Blogger

Birds of a feather flock together.

—The Dictionarie in Spanish and English (1599), which was compiled by the English lexicographer John Minsheu.

Chapter 1

Bartonville

He felt different. More energetic, more alive. He bred with female after female in his flock without tiring. He stayed awake through the night. He feared no predator.

Then a turkey hunter shot him.

The setting sun overlooked a crisp, clear evening in early November. South of Bartonville, Illinois, a farmer had leased his wood lot to two turkey hunters. Big and burly in their bulky camouflaged outfits, they had just bagged one.

"Good shot, Pete!"

"He's a big 'un!"

Pete and Bob walked up to the tom turkey, bleeding on the cold ground. The rest of the flock had scattered into the woods. He had exceptionally good plumage and weighed perhaps twenty pounds. Pete reached down and picked him up by the neck.

"He weighs at least twenty-five pounds!"

Then the turkey's eyes opened—and gleamed red. He kicked with his spurs and pecked savagely at Pete's arms and eyes. Dozens of his hens attacked the men from behind.

"Gobble! Gobble!"

He felt different. More energetic, more alive. He had no memory of being shot, but a certain turkey satisfaction at killing his killers. He also enjoyed pecking at their dead meat. He had always liked frogs, but this meat tasted better. He led his flock down the road, in search of more predators to eat.

* * *

Bill Westcot, the coroner of Midley, Illinois (population 512), had seen his share of grisly deaths, but this one took the cake. Two hunters apparently pecked to death by turkeys. How could this be? Wild turkeys were normally shy and secretive, not even as aggressive as geese. Bill looked up as a man came in—average height, maybe five nine, medium build, not fat, not skinny, roundish face, hazel eyes, and brown hair. He would be hard to remember. But Bill had known him all his life.

Sam Melvin, the reporter for *Midley Beacon*, dropped in for his daily chat. Sam and Bill had been friends since elementary school, and they had both stayed around Midley all their lives. Bill, a short, stocky guy with blondish hair, had gone off to school and become a coroner.

Sam had stayed in Midley after high school, doing odd jobs, until he got on with the *Midley Beacon*. As a reporter and blogger for a small-town weekly paper, Sam wasn't especially busy, and he liked to socialize.

When he saw what remained of the corpses on the mortuary slabs, Sam exclaimed, "Gowlurp! Gaawka-urop!" He ran to the bathroom and puked. After washing out his mouth, he returned, eyes averted.

"Who in the hell were those poor bastards?"

"Peter James and Robert Smithville, according to their drivers' licenses and their shooting permits."

"They look like someone went at them with a thousand pickaxes."

"Yup. Pretty gruesome, even for me."

"What in the world happened?"

"As far as I can tell, they were pecked to death by a flock of wild turkeys."

"I've never heard of anything like that!"

"Yeah, that's not really normal turkey behavior."

"Could they be rabid?"

"Turkeys don't get rabid, Sam."

"They don't attack hunters either. Is 'death by wild turkey' what you'll put on their death certificates?"

"Yeah, I guess so."

"Well, that's what I'll put as my story headline then. It'll be in tomorrow's paper."

"Make sure when you write it up, people know that 'wild turkey' is a bird and not liquor."

"How can you joke when you have these poor fellows on the slab over there?"

"It's a job. You get used to it."

* * *

He led his flock in the evenings and mornings across the woods and fields. They rested during the day. They did not encounter any more predators. If he'd been human, he would have sighed. They settled for their normal forage, as well as small amphibians. They met a couple of other flocks of wild turkeys. He defeated their toms and took their hens. His flock numbered over a hundred now.

He smelled something on the wind. Turkeys. He headed that way, leading his flock.

* * *

Leaning on the gate to his barn, Amos Yoder, owner of Yoder Turkey Farms, looked over his turkeys with pride. He raised over ten thousand turkeys, all fed on non-GMO grain that he grew himself. His internet business was booming. He was even selling turkeys on Amazon! Selling organically fed turkeys over the internet had led to him buying a Cadillac and motor home with cash after growing up on the family turkey farm. All he had to do was keep the turkeys clean and comfortable and fed.

A life of hard physical labor had given him arms thick as a chuck roast. People always thought of him as taller than he was because of his broad chest and big head. Most of the time, he took things as they came. In trouble or opposition, he was an immovable rock.

Behind him he heard the "Gobble! Gobble!" of a turkey. He thought one had slipped out of the other gate in the barn. Turning around quickly, his mouth dropped. Over a hundred wild turkeys were running at him! A big tom with a reddish stain on his breast led the charge. Their bright-red eyes chilled Amos's blood.

"Gobble! Gobble!"

Slipping around the gate to the barn, he grabbed his gun. Aiming carefully, he shot the tom in the breast. He dropped

3

like a stone. The remaining turkeys continued in a wave toward the gate, flying up and bouncing off the heavy mesh used to keep the turkeys in. "Gobble! Gobble!" they screamed in futility.

Amos smiled smugly. "That'll keep them out." But the tom stood up. He wobbled a little and led the flock to the other side of the barn.

"I swore I hit him!" Amos put down the .22 long rifle he'd used. In the office he pulled his shotgun out of the gun safe. "Let's see how he handles a shotgun blast! At least I won't miss with this." He ran to the gate at the other end of the barn. The turkeys flew up, trying to peck their way through the mesh.

"It's like Hitchcock's *The Birds*," Amos grumbled. "But they didn't have a pump-action shotgun in that movie."

He cracked open a door and blasted them. Three or four turkeys exploded in a spray of blood and feathers. But the rest didn't flee in panic. They turned as one and charged toward the door. *BLAM! BLAM! BLAM! BLAM!* As fast as he could pump, Amos fired shell after shell of 00 shot into them. Over two dozen fell into piles of shredded meat. Then the first ones he'd blasted stood up. The turkeys' exposed muscle glistened red with blood, with entrails hanging down and dragging on the ground—but they hopped and staggered toward him.

He was so dumbfounded—the turkeys actually reached the door. *BLAM!* Three more birds turned to turkey burger. Click. Out of ammo. He tried to slam the door—but the big tom blocked him. He had blood all over his breast, but he pecked and kicked with his spurs like a demon.

"Ow!" Amos slammed the butt of the shotgun into the turkey with a satisfying crunch. Three turkeys flew through the open door and landed on his face. Spurs gouged his cheeks and eyes. He thrashed wildly, but dozens more piled on. A pile of pecking, kicking, gouging turkeys soon buried him.

"Gobble! Gobble!"

The mound under the feeding turkeys twitched and was still.

* * *

He felt strong, powerful. He now had many more hens with which to breed. So he went to it immediately.

The turkeys only had one door ajar into the barn, but as dozens and hundreds and thousands joined the flock, the weight of them sprung the door completely open. They found other predators around the barn and dispatched them. They spotted the grain silos and feasted. They continued into the woods and fields around the barns, ever expanding their territory.

* * *

"What?" Sam Melvin exclaimed as he read the *Normal Shout*'s story about the mysterious death at Yoder's turkey farm and the disappearance of ten thousand turkeys.

"Keep it down," growled Lisa Kambacher, his boss and the editor of the *Midley Beacon*, and the only other employee at the small weekly newspaper. "I'm busy editing your crap."

Sam swiveled his ancient, uncomfortable office chair from his laptop so he faced Lisa. He'd garbage-picked that chair from his neighbor in Midley when he was hired fifteen years ago. Her thin face, framed in brown hair, peered at the computer screen.

Lisa's dark-brown eyes stared intently at what she edited. Maybe it was the piece Sam had written about Mrs. Huntington and her award-winning afghans. He hadn't enjoyed reporting that; he couldn't imagine she'd like editing it.

"Drop that story and put in this one. The crap has really hit the fan now. Remember the grisly deaths of those turkey hunters I wrote about last week?"

"Yeah. That was a great story. We sold out that edition and had to run another five hundred copies." Lisa looked up from her computer.

"It looks like that flock of killer turkeys is now ten thousand or more."

"That *is* a good story. Where are they?"

"No one knows."

"Well, go out and find them! Oh, and write a story connecting the two occurrences before you go. Maybe we'll publish a special 'Killer Turkey' edition. It will be very appropriate for November, between Halloween and

Thanksgiving." She smiled hopefully. "Maybe that one will sell out too! I could use a new laptop."

"I want some hazard pay for this story."

"OK, I'll give you an extra hundred bucks if you come back with the turkeys' location. Oh, and take a shotgun."

"Fat lot of good that did for poor Amos Yoder. He emptied six shells from his, and he still got henpecked to death." Sam shook his head sadly.

"What could they tell from the dead turkeys they found?"

"That's one more weird thing: there were no dead turkeys. They found lots of blood, 00 buckshot, and his bloody corpse."

"That's good stuff. Write it all up and hightail it out of here," Lisa urged.

After typing up his story and sending it to Lisa for editing, he stared at her.

Because of his good grades, Sam's high school English teacher had suggested he volunteer for the school paper. He'd gone to the newspaper "office," a walk-in closet, and had seen a tall, slender girl pounding away on an old IBM PC. She'd looked up sharply, scowled, and said, "What do you want? Do you have a story?"

"Uh, um, I'd like to work for the newspaper."

"Hmmm. I could use a reporter. Let me test you out. There's a track meet today after school. Go to it. Get all the winners and losers and their *feelings*. Our readers care about them. Write it up, and report back to me here by seven p.m."

"You'll still be here at that time?" Sam asked incredulously.

"Of course. I'm the editor and head reporter and writer. I've got twenty stories to write, and I've got to report on the tennis match after school today. I expect you to work just as hard, if you want to stay on."

"Uh, OK."

"What's your name, anyway?"

"Sam Melvin."

"Sam, I'm Lisa Kambacher. Do what I say, and we'll get along fine. Cross me, and you'll regret it for the rest of your life!"

Sam had later learned that after she'd graduated from college, Lisa had started the *Midley Beacon*, the town's first newspaper and one of the first online newspapers in the '90s. Amazingly, by pinching pennies, she'd actually been able to keep it going these past fifteen years.

Sam sighed. Shaking off his reverie, he pulled up a map on his laptop and studied central Illinois. The turkey hunters were killed west of the Illinois River and south of Bartonville. Yoder's turkey farm sat between Hanna City and Smithville. So the wild turkeys had traveled about fifteen miles during that week. They went northwest through farms and scrub. From Yoder's farm they had a clear shot due north to the several square miles of wilderness surrounding the Wildlife Prairie Park. Sam guessed they would avoid built-up areas and travel by night, roosting among trees during the day. Central Illinois was pretty sparsely settled, and even a flock of ten thousand turkeys could hide in the many wooded creeks and valleys.

The Yoder farm had been attacked yesterday. If the turkeys moved two miles a day, they'd arrive in the park in about two or three days. Sam drew a circle of four miles around the turkey farm. He'd spend the day circling around it.

* * *

Most of the day Sam drove up and down Illinois 116 and Taylor Road. The sun shone brightly, making the November day surprisingly warm. He used his binoculars to look across the fallow fields of November to the tree line of the nearest creek—Johnson Run.

He drove around Greengold Road and Murphy Road, and stopped and talked with the people of Hanna City. They were pretty upset over Amos Yoder's death. The townspeople knew and liked Amos since he had grown up in the area. People in central Illinois were pretty stable; they tended to live and work in or near the towns where they grew up.

Sam stopped at the office of the *Hanna City Monitor*, the town's paper, to trade what the *Monitor*'s reporters had found with what he knew about the story. It was twice the size of the *Midley Beacon*'s one-room rental on the Main Street of Midley. It had better furniture too.

"Hi, Sam Melvin of the *Midley Beacon*."

"Hi, Sam. I'm James Appleby, the feature's reporter. What can I do for you?" said a middle-aged man with gray-and-brown hair. "Have a seat." He gestured to a spare chair.

Sitting, Sam said, "I've been following these turkey attacks since last week when we had two hunters killed in Bartonville. What can you tell me about the attack on Yoder's turkey farm?"

"You don't say? Well, poor Amos's body, or what was left of it, was discovered by a truck driver dropping off supplies for the farm. The attack apparently had taken place at about seven a.m. in the morning. His wife, Helen, had already left for town, where she teaches third grade." He paused. "I didn't know about the deaths of those turkey hunters. What can you tell me?"

"They were hunting turkeys that evening and were pecked to death. Here's a printout of our news story and our website. Go ahead and use it and cite us as your source."

"Thanks. I'll be sure to link to your original story."

Sam looped around to the south of Hanna City and drove to Yoder Turkey Farms. He slammed his car door in the driveway and headed toward the nearest building. The grounds were neat and tidy, with white fences and white trim on the dark-green barn, but the barn doors gaped open. The turkeys had left, but their smell remained. A dark, wet area stained the ground in front of a sprung door. That must be where Amos Yoder had died, Sam thought.

"Can I help you?"

Sam turned around and saw a middle-aged woman looking at him. She had light-brown hair with a few gray streaks. She looked like she would be a fine grandmother in a few years. Her eyes were weary and her face haggard though.

"Hi. I'm Sam Melvin, reporter from the *Midley Beacon*. Are you Mrs. Yoder?"

"Yes."

"My condolences, ma'am. I can't imagine how you feel."

"Thank you. I'm a little numb. It doesn't seem real. It's like something in a book." She rubbed her hands up and down her arms, as if chilled.

"Yes. I can understand if you don't want to talk. Are you able to answer a few questions?"

"I'll try."

Sam flipped to a blank page on his reporter's notebook. "Was there anyone else on the farm at the time?"

"Yes. Fred Jones and Harry Bishop were working here. They're as dead as poor Amos."

"You don't say! I hadn't heard that."

"The truck driver found Amos, and I got notified. Later, the police found the others. I was completely out of it yesterday."

"I understand. I read that Amos's shotgun had been used."

"Yes. At least he went down with a fight. He also shot his .22 rifle. The police found that in his office, and his gun safe open."

"The most puzzling thing is there were no turkey bodies found."

"Not exactly."

"What do you mean?"

"The police found pieces of turkey scattered around the barn gate, just as you'd expect from a shotgun, but no bodies."

"What do you think happened to them?"

"I don't know. Maybe the turkeys ate them."

"But why would they leave behind scraps?"

"I don't know, Mr. Melvin. I don't know how I'm going to live. I've lost Amos, I've lost the turkeys, and I'll probably lose the farm!" Tears trickled down her cheeks.

Sam uncomfortably put his arm around the crying woman. "Do you have any insurance?"

"I don't know!" She sobbed and then hiccupped. "I think so. I know Amos had life insurance. But he ran the business! I teach school and decorate the house and then do gardening!" She cried again.

"Um, did anyone know Amos's business affairs?"

She stopped crying. "Yes—his insurance agent, Zo Limbach. I could call him."

"Good idea."

"Would you mind leaving now?"

"Thank you for your time Mrs. Yoder. God bless you."

"Thank you for your help. Good-bye." Sam looked around. It was a big farm. Down two hands, the owner, and ten thousand turkeys. He didn't know how she was going to live either.

* * *

He felt great. He was full of energy, he had many hens to breed with, and he was the leader of a great flock. The flock stayed close to the woods and streams. They rested now, in and under the trees by the river. In the evening he'd lead them upstream. That felt like the right direction.

Chapter 2

Edwards

As the day ended, Sam headed back north. Farm fields covered the area south of Hanna City. There were more streams and woods north of Route 116. He went back along Murphy Road to Greengold Road. He stopped at a random house, where a man was raking and burning leaves.

A heavyset man walked up to Sam's car as he rolled down his window.

"Hi," Sam said.

"Hi. Are you lost?" asked the man, with straight dark hair, wearing a plaid flannel shirt and jeans.

"Ha, no, but I'm looking for something."

"What's that? Nearest fillin' station is on Farmington road."

"This is going to sound crazy..."

"Try me."

"Have you noticed any flocks of turkeys around here?"

"You're right. It does sound crazy. We have some turkeys in the woods along Johnson Run, but you only see them in the morning and evening."

Consulting the map he had printed out back in Midley, Sam said, "Hmm, I guess I should just follow Murphy Road north. My name's Sam Melvin, by the way. I'm a reporter for the *Midley Beacon*." He handed the man his business card.

"Name's George Rivers. Pleased to meetcha. You're a ways from home. Are you on a wild turkey chase?"

"Sort of. First, wild turkeys in Bartonville killed two hunters. Then they attacked a turkey farm in Hanna City. I thought they might be up this way."

"You mean Yoder's turkey farm? I heard Amos got kilt, but I didn't know how."

"He got killed all right, by turkeys. All ten thousand of his flock have escaped. I thought someone might have seen something."

"Ten thousand turkeys on the loose!" George whistled. "That'd be something. You might as well look now, now that it's dark. Those white turkeys will stand out like sheets on a clothesline at night."

The sun settled below the horizon. Just a red glow remained in the west. The first stars appeared in the deepening blue.

"OK. I'll take off then. Wish me luck!"

"OK. I guess I'll read about it in the paper."

Sam drove rapidly along the country roads heading north. He scanned left and right, but saw nothing. He parked his car and used his binoculars, looking for any movement under the trees. Nothing. He drove all the way north of Wildlife Prairie Park to Route 8 and then came back south along Taylor Road. Nothing. The clock on the dash showed ten. He headed to his motel.

Just before he got to Route 116, he saw something on the road. At first, he thought it a small herd of deer. Then he saw dozens of white turkeys. Then hundreds. Then thousands. They crossed the road from west to east, from the woods to the open fields. He slowed and stopped. Among the thousands of white turkeys were a few dark wild turkeys. Some ran, some walked.

A thump shook the car. Then another. A wild turkey pecked at Sam's windshield, right in front of his face. Shockingly, the windshield cracked.

"Enough of this!" Sam gunned the engine. He'd always liked powerful luxury cars, but he couldn't afford them new. His antique 1981 Lincoln Town Car had a four-hundred-and-eighty-cubic-inch engine with over four hundred horsepower. The turkeys attacking the car flew off. He hit sixty-five when he smashed into the main flock. Splat! Splat! Splat! Dozens of turkeys bounced off the car, crunching and bursting like giant, blood-filled water balloons. The crack in the windshield spread all the way across.

"Crap. That's another three hundred bucks for a new windshield. At least I got some of the buggers for you, Amos."

Sam drove straight to Hanna City, town of twelve hundred. He reported his turkey sighting to the police there.

"I'm Sam Melvin with the *Midley Beacon*. You know those ten thousand turkeys from Yoder's farm?"

"Yes?" said the desk sergeant, whose name tag read *Rich Randolph*. The sergeant looked at Sam through dark eyes. His thinning hair combed straight back framed his rectangular face.

"I found them a quarter mile north of 116, crossing Taylor Road, headed northeast."

"Thank you, Mr. Melvin. We'll send a car to investigate."

"Be careful. Those turkeys are killers."

"We know. We investigated the Yoder farm."

"I hit a couple dozen of them with my car. Maybe you can bring in some samples."

Sergeant Randolph made a note. "We'll do that."

"Here's my card. Let me know if you find out anything about the turkeys."

Back in his car, Sam called Lisa.

"Whatcha want?" She snarled her greeting.

"Hi, Lisa. I know it's late, but I found the turkeys!"

"It's about time! It's nearly midnight! It took you all day? Anyway, email me the story tonight. I can update the edition and have it printed tomorrow morning. I'll print a whole thousand!"

"Will do."

"Good job. That's a hundred bucks for you, Sam, for your hazard pay."

"Great!" Sam said. "Now I only need two hundred more for my windshield."

"Put it on the paper's expense account, Sam."

"Wow. Thanks." This was the first time Lisa had ever let him expense anything.

"Just a business expense of the paper. Turkey damaged windshield. Note it in the expense description on your trip report. Then we can deduct it on our income tax—assuming we have income this year. Later." Lisa hung up.

"Bye," Sam said to the silent phone. That was a normal "good-bye" for Lisa.

Compliments from Lisa were rare, like less than annual. He tried to think of the last one he'd received. He thought it was last year, at Christmastime, when he'd gone in to Peoria to report on a Jonas Brothers' concert at the Peoria Civic Center. He'd worked Christmas Eve, and Lisa'd included it in the paper's Christmas edition. She was trying to appeal to millennials with the *Beacon*'s online paper, so the article was important for her campaign. She also got free tickets from the Jonas Brothers' publicist, which she used as a promotion for their paper—given to whoever got the most subscriptions, online or paper. After their Christmas paper sold out, she'd said "Good job" then too.

Back in high school, he remembered she had been rougher. One time she'd said, "Why the hell haven't you gotten that story done yet, Sam?"

"Uh, it's just twenty minutes since I came from the ball game."

"The paper's due out *tonight*! Twenty minutes is twice as much time as you need, you lazy nebbish!"

"You're just nitpicking!"

"That's good in an editor! That's why I'm the editor and you're the lazy reporter I have to flog to get to work!"

After he'd finished typing up the story and handed her the floppy, he looked up the word *nebbish*. Lisa had an overwhelming vocabulary and loved using it. She enjoyed insulting people without them realizing it. The dictionary defined *nebbish* as "a person, especially a man, who is regarded as pitifully ineffectual, timid, or submissive." Huh. He had to admit that was pretty accurate. Aside from English and the newspaper, he hadn't really ever done anything. And he was a follower.

A compliment in those days was when Lisa *didn't* insult him over a story he had written. Sam had learned to use Lisa's vocabulary in the stories he wrote. She didn't criticize those stories.

Sam kind of liked Lisa despite her badgering. She picked on him and everyone else all the time, so it wasn't like she especially disliked him. Most of the time, her criticism was spot on—which was why most people, especially girls, hated her.

Sam stopped at the first hotel he came to. He quickly typed up his story and emailed it to Lisa. It was 1:00 a.m., and he was tired. He hit the sack.

* * *

The next morning Sam went into the police station to see what the police had learned during the night. The desk sergeant, May Callahan, looked up from her desk. A square woman in her late twenties or early thirties, with auburn hair, her blue eyes looked directly at Sam.

"Hi. Sam Melvin from the *Midley Beacon*. I talked with Sergeant Randolph last night, and he said they would send a squad car to Taylor Road to investigate the turkey flock that killed Amos Yoder. Do you have an updated report?"

She consulted her papers. "Yes, the report from the squad car said there was blood on the road and a few parts of turkeys. No whole bodies though. You're the guy who drove through that flock with a car?"

"Yeah, and I've got the cracked windshield to prove it."

"You'd better get that fixed. My brother does windshields, right here in town—Callahan's Auto Repair. Anyway, the patrol officer found no other signs of the turkey flock."

"Wow. I'm sure I killed at least a dozen of the buggers. I might as well get my windshield repaired. They've probably settled down during the day. I'll go looking for them again tonight."

* * *

He felt great, full of energy. He'd led his huge flock over the river, through the woods, over the fields, and back into the woods. He followed creeks and rivers along the way.

There was a predator in front of the flock. They attacked and killed it. Then another. Then another. This was a good location for feeding! They found a cave full of food. They ate it. Other caves contained predators they could not reach.

The flock was full of food. It was dark. They rested in the woods until the morning.

* * *

Soon after sunset, Sergeant Callahan called Sam.

15

"Sam Melvin?"

"Yes?"

"This is May Callahan. We just got a report of a turkey attack at the Wildlife Prairie Park this evening. We sent a squad car to investigate."

"Thanks for the tip, May! I'll be right there!"

"No problem. I like to keep my brother's customers happy and maintain good communication with the press."

Sam called Lisa using his Bluetooth headset as he drove over to Wildlife Prairie Park.

"Hi, Lisa."

"What's up, Sam?"

"We've got another turkey attack, this time at the Wildlife Prairie Park."

"That's odd."

"Why?"

"I thought they'd avoid the park due to the people and predators there."

"They haven't exactly avoided people so far. Maybe they think people are food."

"That's true. Well, find out what the turkeys are up to, write your story, and send it in tonight. I'll put out another paper tomorrow, and of course, there's the website to update."

"Will do."

"'Night, Sam."

"Good night, Lisa."

Wildlife Prairie Park was already closed when he got there, but Sam could see the police car from Hanna City in the drive. He drove around the closed gates, looking for someone to talk to. He noted the lit-up gift shop. Entering it, he saw a policeman and a security guard talking.

"Hi. Sam Melvin from the *Midley Beacon*."

"Hi, Sam. I've heard of you. I'm Officer Patrick O'Reily from Hanna City. I'm the one who went to Taylor Road last night, after you tipped us off."

"Hi, Patrick." They shook hands. Sam looked at the security guard.

"Matt Funk. I handle security for the park at night."

"Hi, Matt. So what have the turkeys done now?"

"The turkeys were in the fox house," Matt said.

"And the wolves' den," Patrick added.

"And the gift shop," Matt continued.

"Busy turkeys! Can you give the story to me in time order?"

"Sure," Matt said. "About six p.m. this evening, after my shift had started and it had gotten dark, I was walking the grounds, checking on the animals, when I got to the red fox's pen—or what was left of the red fox."

"What was left?"

"Just the coat. The animal had been pecked to death. There were turkey feathers all around."

"That sounds familiar."

"I checked on other animals. The wolves were also dead, eviscerated and eaten. The other animals looked OK."

"Could you show me?"

"Sure."

Sam looked carefully at the fox carcass and the ground around it. He found some turkey parts: a leg here, a head there, and a lot of feathers. It was the same at the wolves' den. Looking at the other animals using his flashlight, he noticed the cuts on the bear's face. There was also blood on its muzzle—and turkey feathers on the ground.

"It looks like the bear fought them off—and maybe ate a couple."

"I never noticed that!" Matt exclaimed.

"Me neither," Patrick said.

"What about the gift shop?"

"When I came back from the checking on the animals," Matt said, "I noticed the gift shop door was open. Something broke the screen and window. Again, there were a lot of turkey feathers around. I saw they had ravaged the snack bar. All the popcorn and candy, crackers, and cookies were gone that had been out for display and sale. There was nothing left but torn wrappers, boxes, and feathers on the floor."

"Wow. You're a really lucky man, Matt."

"Why?"

"The last two guys to run into these turkeys ended up looking like the fox and wolves."

Matt looked stunned and at a loss for words.

"Thanks for your help, Matt and Patrick. If you ever sight any more zombie turkeys, let me know. Here's my card."

Sam left for his motel in Hanna City. There he typed up the story and sent it to Lisa and got to sleep. He would look for the turkeys again early tomorrow morning.

* * *

He felt great, full of energy. He led his flock out of the woods. Now there was another field in front of them, with a large barnlike structure on it. Maybe it was another turkey barn! He'd go free them and gain more members for his flock. They had acquired more wild turkey flocks during their march. Now twelve thousand strong, they charged the barnlike structure.

* * *

The Caterpillar Edwards Dealer Education facility was preparing for a big customer demonstration. A large 390F backhoe was digging trenches and D-11 and D-10 tractors were filling them in—inside the voluminous demonstration building. It was only 7:30 a.m., but they had a scripted and choreographed performance to practice, showing the capabilities of the company's huge machines.

Part of script was for the 390s to dig a huge trench, have a small D-4 tractor go into it and smooth it out, and then have the big D-11s fill it back in.

Then an enormous flock of turkeys entered through the open arena door. "Gobble! Gobble!"

That was not in the script.

The turkeys were mostly white, with some dark gray and brown ones mixed in. They flew up to the people directing the machines on the floor and began pecking them.

Hurt and bleeding, they ran yelling to the office door.

"Those turkeys are crazy!"

"And they all have those bright-red eyes too. Creepy."

"There're still more outside!"

"Close the doors then!" And they closed the doors. There were still perhaps a thousand turkeys walking and flying around the demonstration area.

The machine operators were relatively secure in their enclosed cabs, although turkeys would fly up and peck at the windows. The tough glass, designed to resist construction debris, foiled the turkeys. All the operators had headsets by which they could speak and hear each other and what the director said. From inside the office, he said, "Go ahead and make the trench. Make it narrower, just one bucket wide."

Operating from opposite ends of the arena, the excavators made a trench a hundred feet long, about eight feet deep, and four feet wide.

"Now, you D-11 operators, push the turkeys into the trench."

With their huge twenty-foot blades of steel, over eight feet high, they pushed clumps of turkeys into the trench. Tangled together, in a narrow space, they couldn't get out again.

"Cover them up!" Thousands of pounds of dirt filled the trench. The hundred-ton dozers ran back and forth over it until it was as solid as the rest of the ground.

"Woowee! We did it!" The operators jumped out and high-fived each other. The script directors came out of the office to celebrate. After the celebration had calmed down, they heard a peculiar sound: *ploop*! And then another: *ploop*! And then *ploop, ploop, ploop*!

They turned around to where the trench had been. Like gigantic bubbles coming out of a swamp, the turkeys were popping up out of the ground. Hundreds were bursting out every second. They looked worse for wear: brown, dirty, with broken legs and wings, but they were hopping and walking and trying to fly anyway. And their eyes were still bright red. They slowly staggered toward the men, dragging broken legs or wings. "Gobble! Gobble!"

"Let's get out of here!" The men ran to the office. One called 911. Another opened the arena door.

"Why are you letting more of those things in?" shouted a worker who'd peeked his head out the office door.

"No, I'm opening it to get them out. Once they've rejoined their flock and the arena is empty, I'll close the doors."

The man who called 911 spoke with May Callahan of the Hanna City police department.

"We're under attack by a crazed flock of turkeys here!"

"Where are you?"

"At the Edwards demonstration area."

"So that's where they went. They were at Wildlife Prairie Park last night."

"They attacked us while we were practicing our script with our machines. We buried them in the dirt, and then they popped right back up out of the ground."

"That's a new one. We'll send a squad car right over."

While waiting for his windshield to be prepared, Sam's phone chirped.

"Hello?" Sam said.

"Hi, Sam. May Callahan. Here's some breaking news for you—the turkeys have landed. They're at the Edwards demonstration area. Do you know where that is?"

"Sure do. I went to Power Parade there with my parents in 1988."

"Be careful. Apparently if you bury them with tractors, they pop back up."

"Huh. I know if you shoot them with a .22 or a shotgun, or hit them with a car, they keep on ticking. I'll be right there. I wonder if there'll finally be any dead birds?"

"Good question. I'll send the forensics team over."

Before he left Callahan's Auto repair, Sam set up his laptop, typed up a story, and emailed it. He also called Lisa.

"Big news, Lisa. The turkeys have landed—at the Edwards Demo Center!"

"I trust you're going to get me a news story on it?"

"Already in the mail!"

"Good. Our thousand copies sold out, and we're also selling the story to the *Peoria Journal Star*, the *Pekin Daily Times*, the *Normal Shout*, and the *Bloomington Bugle*. Further, AP has paid for your stories too. You're the only reporter covering this story so far! But the big names from Chicago and New York will be coming in soon, so keep working!"

"Wow. I never thought I'd be famous."

"I wouldn't be surprised if Oprah invited you to her show."

"I didn't know she had a show anymore."

"Yeah, it's just on her OWN network. Stay on your toes. I want you to stay ahead of our competition."

"I will. Nobody knows zombie turkeys up close and personal like me."

"Zombie turkeys! What a great name! I'll use that in today's headline."

"Today's? Are we having a special edition?"

"Yeah, I'll publish daily as long as this story keeps developing."

"Wow, that's the first time Midley has ever had a daily newspaper."

"Yeah, makes ya proud to be part of the two that publish it."

"Lisa, we're finally hitting it big time."

"Fifteen years after high school. Persistence pays."

"Gotta go. Got some zombie turkeys to catch."

"Get photos and video!"

"OK. Bye."

Sam arrived at the Cat demo center just as the forensics team was unpacking their van. They went into the demonstration arena. The long trench in the middle of the arena was pockmarked with hundreds of turkey-sized holes. Blood darkened the dirt. Using a small excavator, they slowly reexcavated the trench. The found pieces and parts: legs, wings, even heads. But no bodies. Then, at the very bottom, they found some mashed turkeys. "Mashed" in the sense of mashed potatoes. They gathered up about ten buckets of mashed turkey and dirt.

"We'll send tissue samples to the Northwestern University's Turkey Institute," the forensics team told Sam.

"I've never heard of a turkey institute."

"Yes, they're kind of a Mayo Clinic of turkey biology, the best in the world. They should be able to figure out what's going on with these crazy turkeys."

"Wow. You learn something new every day. Here's my business card. Call me if you learn anything else."

Sam got out his trusty laptop. Where would the turkeys go next? Jubilee State Park was the next big undeveloped area. He drove there.

His search repeated his experience by Hanna City. No signs of turkeys, and none of the people he talked with knew anything. He drove around to the east and west and saw nothing of the turkeys. He did see news vans from the local TV stations. He followed them back to Edwards to see if they had any tips. They were just getting the story at the demonstration center; they didn't have any more news.

Frustrated and tired, he traveled to Dunlap and stayed in a cheap motel. He had a hunch the turkeys roosted in Jubilee Park, and he wanted to explore early the next morning.

He woke up at 4:00 a.m., had a quick muffin at the breakfast bar, and hit the road toward Jubilee Park. He turned on the police scanner in case the police broadcast anything.

Then he heard of the attack in Princeville.

Chapter 3

Princeville

Jimmy Manheim picked up the packages for his delivery in Princeville, a small town of less than two thousand people, where he went to high school. He delivered the packages for a national package delivery service. The job gave him a little extra income to pay for the gas in his car. After delivering to ten houses, he saw a flock of turkeys cross the road. A really *big* flock. The continual high pitched "Gobble! Gobble!" sounded eerie rising from the flock in the cool morning air. He had heard about some sort of turkey problem in Hanna City and Kickapoo; were they now in Princeville?

Then several stopped and turned to face him. Their eyes gleamed blood red. Some marched toward him. Make that a *lot* marched toward him. "Gobble! Gobble!" He put the car in reverse, did a J-turn, and hightailed it back to downtown Princeville. He headed east on IL-90, ignoring the speed laws until he got to the police station.

The policeman at the desk, Officer Simpkins, a man with a buzz cut and a bullet-shaped head, took Jimmy's report seriously and immediately radioed the PD's only squad car to go west on IL-90.

On his way, policeman Earl Boyd heard gunshots coming from a farmhouse off IL-90.

Thousands of turkeys surrounded the house, and someone from inside fired a shotgun at them. When Earl pulled into the drive, the turkeys left the house and headed for the police car, swarming over it. "Gobble! Gobble!"

"What the hell!" exclaimed Officer Boyd as he backed up, smashing dozens of turkeys with the powerful engine of his LTD, and headed east toward town. The zombie turkeys followed him into Princeville.

Vince Thorn was chopping wood early in the morning, when the turkeys came upon him. "Gobble! Gobble!" they called by the hundreds as they flew over his fence. He whaled on them with his axe, dispatching several of them. More and more swarmed at him. He used his baseball-hitting skills to get the ones going for his face, but they encircled him, attacking him from the back and sides. Running into his tool shed, he got his chainsaw started and stood at the door, mowing them down as they came at him. This went on for about fifteen minutes, long enough for him to build a three-foot wall of sawn turkey pieces in front of him. As suddenly as the turkeys came, they left, although the remaining corpses had the annoying habit of getting back up and staggering toward him. In this way he learned he had to saw them cleanly in half to kill them for good.

"Gobble! Gobble!"

Hundreds of turkeys got into Princeville's Piggley Wiggley grocery store through the cart return door. Most of the early-morning shoppers fled in panic. The manager, John Friedling, used a fire extinguisher to good effect, both in spraying and suffocating them and in bashing them over their heads. Another employee chopped them up using a fire axe in the frozen-food section. The resident butcher chimed in with his largest cleaver. Blood spattered everywhere. When the turkeys had been driven from the store and the manager thought the attack had been thwarted, the corpses arose. Back came the axe and the cleaver. This time they made sure the pieces were bite sized.

"Phew! I just about lost it when they got up again," John said.

"Yeah, some didn't even have their heads," Nathan Block, the butcher replied.

"At least that made them easier to kill—again. They ran around like turkeys with their heads cut off."

"Uh-oh," Nathan said.

"Now what?"

"Look in the fresh turkey section, in the cooler over there."

Under the *Fresh Turkeys for Thanksgiving* sign, struggling to get out of their plastic wrappings, which had been pierced by turkey spurs during the battle, the fresh turkeys wriggled in the refrigerator. All had been covered in blood from the zombie turkeys. One managed to get free of the string wrapped around its legs and lay on its back, vigorously waving the stumps of its legs in the air. Headless, footless, it looked ridiculous—like a turkey-sized slug. Even as they watched, the wings started waving, and the stumps of the drumsticks sprouted buds, which blossomed into feet. Black dots appeared all over the turkeys, which began growing into feathers. A head was slowly sprouting from the chopped neck.

CHOP! Nathan split one from stem to stern. Fresh giblets flew everywhere.

CHOP! John hacked one in half with the fire axe. After dispatching the other wrigglers, John said, "I guess they're past their expiration date. I don't think we can sell these."

Warren Zapp, a Gulf War veteran, returned home from the nightshift at Caterpillar that morning. He bent his broad back and picked up his morning paper, the *Midley Beacon*, on his way into his house, when he heard "Gobble! Gobble!" from hundreds of turkeys flying into his yard. He quickly ducked into his house and slammed the door on them. Thump! Thump! Scores of turkeys hit the doors and windows like gigantic, paranormal hail.

"That's enough of that!" he said grimly to himself. He went into his basement and got his somewhat illegal AK-47 that he had captured in Baghdad during the war in 2003. He had plenty of ammo too. He lifted the second story window and opened fire on the hundreds of turkeys in his yard.

"I suppose this counts as a predation permit," he said as he reloaded a fifty-round drum. "Not sure the police would approve it within the city limits. That's fine. They can come arrest me."

Dozens of Warren's neighbors had already called the police, and not just because of the shooting of the automatic weapon. They too had hundreds of turkeys in their yards.

The police, however, were busy fighting the turkeys in the town square with shotguns, handguns, and rifles. The turkeys went down by the hundreds—and slowly came back up, bloody but unbowed and undeterred.

After Warren had cleared his yard for the second time and saw the turkeys rising yet again, he raged.

"No you don't. You don't defeat a US Marine that easily." He went into his attached garage and filled mason jars and old liquor bottles with gas. He tore up a shirt and put a strip of cloth in each, screwing it on with the top. When he had several dozen, he went back to his second-floor window, lit the gas-soaked cloths, and threw them at the turkeys. Each exploded into a ball of flame when it hit, splashing them with flaming gasoline.

Fire and being burned alive got through to the turkeys. They left his yard, even the resurrected ones that were not much more than bleeding balls of feathers.

"Oho! You don't like that? There's more where that came from!" He took his remaining jars, slid into his pickup truck, and followed the flock to the town square. Perhaps three or four thousand turkeys gathered there, attacking a line of police who were blazing away at them with shotguns, pistols, and rifles. It looked like a standoff: thousands of turkeys on one side of the square, a dozen policemen on the other.

The back of his truck held a metal tool box and picnic cooler in addition to his Molotov cocktails. He filled them both with gas from a nearby station. Then he backed his truck into the flock of turkeys and stopped suddenly, dumping out the cooler and the tool chest, splashing gallons of gasoline over the turkeys. Then he tossed his Molotov cocktails at them.

Hundreds of turkeys blazed up in flames. Thousands scattered every which way. The zombie turkeys were finally on the run. Maybe the town would reimburse him for his cooler, tool chest, and the gas he bought.

* * *

When Sam pulled into the town square fifteen minutes later, the turkey carcasses were still smoking.

"Wow, it looks like a war zone!" In addition to the burnt turkeys, there were bullet holes everywhere. Plumes of smoke

26

rose here and there. As he interviewed bystanders, they quickly led him to Warren Zapp, a big burly guy, about six feet tall and two twenty. He had long curly blond hair and a scruffy beard.

"Hi. I'm Sam Melvin. You're Warren Zapp?" Sam began when he met him.

"Yeah. Sam Melvin? I've heard of you. You write for the *Midley Beacon*, don't you?"

"Yeah, how'dja know?"

"I just started my subscription this week."

"So it was you who smoked the turkeys?"

"Yeah, good old Molotov cocktails and a Coleman cooler full of gasoline."

"Do you mind if I make a video of you describing how you did this?"

"No problem." Warren described how he fought off the turkeys from his home, first with his AK-47 and then with Molotov cocktails. He finished with his description of flaming the turkeys in the town square.

Sam added questions from behind his cell phone. "So the turkeys came back to life after you shot them?"

"Yeah, but not after they were burned. That's when I decided to do the same thing downtown to the big flock of them there."

"Wasn't the police gunfire effective?"

"Yeah, but they kept getting back up. Once they got into the burning gasoline, that stopped. Fire also seems to scare them."

"Thanks so much, Warren Zapp, US Marine Corps veteran." After he stopped recording the video, Sam said to Warren, "Here's my business card. If you ever have any turkey tips or info, give me a call."

Tracking the path of the turkeys through the town, Sam found the Piggly Wiggly store, thanks to the crowd standing in the parking lot. A hand-painted sign said, *Free Turkeys! Guaranteed Dead!*

Sam chuckled at the gallows humor. He interviewed the store manager, John Friedling, about the battle in the Piggly Wiggly store. Again he recorded his interview on his cell phone.

"So all the fresh turkeys came to life?"

"Yes. It was the grossest thing I've ever seen. The limbs were wriggling inside the plastic wrapping like...like worms, but they were stumps and wings."

"Were they all splashed with blood?"

"Yes. The whole frozen-food aisle was drenched with it."

"What about these turkeys? Why didn't they come to life?" Sam pointed to another refrigerated bin, still splattered with blood.

"Hmm. Those are our brined turkeys."

"Maybe the brine had some disinfectant power."

"That makes sense."

"Keep samples of the turkeys that came to life, the blood, and these brine turkeys. I'll get the forensics guys to send them to the Turkey Institute."

"What's the Turkey Institute?"

"It's the Mayo Clinic of turkey research in the US. Here's my card. Call me if you have any other turkey problems."

After making sure the turkey samples had been captured, Sam called his forensic contacts in Hanna City. Then he continued through town, backtracking the turkeys' path of destruction as he headed west.

He saw another crowd around one house on the outskirts of town. Stopping, he walked around the throng and saw an impressive and grisly pile of turkey parts by a shed.

"Who did that!?" Sam exclaimed.

"I did," replied a short, wiry man with red hair.

"I'm Sam Melvin, reporter for the *Midley Beacon*. How'd you kill so many? Oh, and what's your name, so I get it in my story correctly?"

"I'm Vince Thorn. I was choppin' wood here this morning, when these turkeys attacked."

"You killed them all with your axe?"

"Nah, there was too many of them. I got my trusty chainsaw out and chopped 'em as they came at me at the door."

"Did any of them revive?"

"Yeah, how'dja know that?"

"I've been following these turkeys for over a week now. They're hard to kill and keep killed."

"You can say that again. I had to saw them completely in half to keep them down."

"That's interesting. Could I take a video of you telling your story?"

"Sure. Will it be the evening news?"

"Maybe. I'm going to put it on the *Midley Beacon*'s YouTube channel."

"I've heard of *Midley*'s website, but I never knew they had a YouTube channel too."

"We're getting more famous, since we're the first with the turkey story. Here. Take my business card. Please call me if you ever are attacked again."

Sam recorded his interview, with Vince in front of the bloody pile of turkeys. He took another sample, putting it in a plastic garbage bag. He took that to the forensics team on his way to his hotel. He typed the story and posted his three videos from Princeville to the *Midley* YouTube channel (75 followers) and linked them to his story. He sent the whole thing to Lisa before calling her.

"Hi, Lisa."

"Hi, Sam. I assume you're in Princeville."

"So you heard."

"It's all over the TV stations. I just got your email. Great work! This is the best you've ever done."

"Wow. You've never said anything like that."

"You've never done work like this before. It's world class. I know because I've got people all over the world coming to our page, calling me all the time, day and night. We sold ten thousand copies of our paper today. I'll print two or three times that tomorrow. But we're really raking in the money selling our stories to the AP—I made special arrangements— and big-name newspapers are running them: *Chicago Sun Times*, *New York Times*, *Wall Street Journal*, as well as ABC, MSNBC, CBS, Fox, and CNN. You just spend whatever you need to, to follow this story, and put the bills on the paper's account."

"Thanks, Lisa."

"Do you have any idea where they're going to next?"

"Let's look at my trusty internet map... They pretty much scattered after Warren Zapp used fire against them. They've been sticking to rivers and wooded areas to roost. Just about any way they go out of town, they'll hit some creeks. That'll lead them to the Rock Island Trail Nature Preserve, most likely."

"I'll tip off the police. You get some rest. I want you ahead of the crowd. You find them again tomorrow morning."

"When are you getting sleep?"

"Thanks for asking! I've hired an answering service out of Peoria. I've got a high school kid reading and answering emails—minimum wage, of course. That's giving me six hours of sleep. We're up to three employees! You've been promoted. Your new title is *Investigative Reporter*. No pay increase, of course."

"Wow. Thanks, Lisa."

"You've earned it."

Chapter 4

Henry

Sam awoke at 4:00 a.m. when Lisa called on his cell phone.

"Sam! I had to wake you up. Your zombie turkey videos have gone viral! They've gotten over three million views overnight!"

"Wow! What does that mean to us? Will all those people buy our paper?"

"No, but we can sell advertising on our video channel and charge more for our videos and reports to the major newspapers. Even better, your videos were used by the national TV stations. They're being shown practically every hour on some twenty-four-hour stations. Have the biggest breakfast you can buy this morning, on the paper. Be sure to put it on your trip expense report. We can deduct it from our income tax."

This burst of generosity rendered him speechless for a moment. Then he managed, "Will do! By the way, I don't mind waking up at 4:00 am when it's you."

"Even if it's just work?"

"As long as it's you."

"Aw. You're going to turn me into a mush ball."

Sam hung up, happy. He'd never been so bold with any woman—and she still seemed to like him.

* * *

At the same time, Tom Tuffield, owner of Tom's Turkeys, a farm near the Illinois River valley north of Henry, finished watching the *Midley* zombie turkey videos for about the tenth time. Those zombie turkeys wouldn't get the best of him! He was handy mechanically, and he knew just what to do.

First, he called his brother-in-law Jerry. Then he cleaned out his woodshed. And he gathered all the wooden boxes he had stored in his barn. When his brother-in-law arrived, the real work began.

* * *

The Illinois State Wildlife commissioner, Bill Heinrich, met early that same morning with the Illinois governor, Larry Brooks, at his office in Springfield. Concern painted Bill's jowly face as he began, "I know this sounds overblown, Larry, but these so-called zombie turkeys are a real public health nuisance. We've had six people killed and a dozen injured. We've lost animals at the Wildlife Prairie Park. We've had one turkey farm infected. If any more turkey farms get this infection, you can just multiply the deaths. I'd like you to call out the National Guard to defend the turkey farms in this state and to hunt down and kill these turkeys."

Larry Brooks, his rugged, square face topped by salt-and-pepper hair, looked grim. "Bill, you're right. I'll get in contact with the National Guard general, and we'll go after those turkeys." To his public relations manager, he said, "Florence, schedule a news conference for this afternoon."

Immaculately dressed in blues and grays, Florence Gunderson began making the necessary phone calls.

She'd scheduled many conferences for the governor, but this was the first one about zombie turkeys.

At the 3:00 p.m. news conference, Governor Brooks and General Charles Bagley appeared together. General Bagley's ramrod straight figure and unlined middle-aged face reflected his daily physical training regime.

Governor Brooks began: "Today I've asked General Bagley to bring out the National Guard and hunt down these dangerous zombie turkeys. We've already tragically lost six people, and a dozen others have been injured in the battle of Princeville. This will not stand in our state! The general is taking immediate action. He will review his plans with you now."

General Bagley, taking a laser pointer, gestured toward the screen, displaying a map of central Illinois. "Here is

Princeville. The estimated ten thousand turkeys have scattered into the surrounding fields and woods. They have been following rivers and wooded areas. We've established a cordon around Route 40 on the east, Route 17 and IL-91 in the north, 78 in the west, and IL-90 to the south. We have squadrons of troops searching the area. Specifically, we're using the K-9 corps, containing specially trained turkey dogs, for searching the wooded areas for turkeys. We will use helicopters and night-vision goggles to search for them day and night. When found, they will be eliminated."

Florence Gunderson, the PR manager said, "Governor Brooks and General Bagley will take questions now."

"What weapons will you use against the zombie turkeys?" asked a reporter from the *Chicago Sun Times*.

"We have a variety of automatic weapons at our disposal, as well as fragmentation grenades."

"Will you use flamethrowers? Fire apparently prevents the zombie turkeys from getting back up," queried a reporter from the *New York Times*.

"The officer in charge of the squads will make that call depending upon the tactical situation."

"How about napalm?" Lisa Kambacher, of the *Midley Beacon*, asked.

"That's a rather extreme weapon for a civilian area. That's not called for—at this time."

"When will it be called for?" Lisa prompted.

"When the tactical situation requires it. Next question?"

"Your plan seems great and well informed, General. Did you get your zombie turkey intelligence from civilian sources, like the *Midley Beacon*?" asked the reporter from the *Peoria Journal Star*.

"Our intelligence comes from the Illinois Wildlife agency, as well as military and civilian sources."

"Do you have a plan if the turkeys manage to slip the cordon?" Bonnie Blatt from the *Normal Shout* asked.

"They are turkeys, ma'am. They have no strategy or plan or intelligence. We have a tight, twenty-four-hour surveillance on those roads, from the air and ground. They are not expected to slip past us."

* * *

That day, Sam had spent some frustrating hours looking for turkeys. He listened to the press conference on the radio while he drove. He knew Lisa was there in Springfield; he recognized her voice.

The Princeville region had a lot of wooded areas for the turkeys to hide.

Driving back to Princeville, Sam saw a biker struggling as he pumped along the Rock Island bike trail next to the road.

"Can I give you a lift?" Sam offered.

"Yeah." He got off his bike and wearily walked it to the back of Sam's Town Car.

"I'm Sam Melvin of the *Midley Beacon*. Did you have an accident? You're bleeding!" Sam exclaimed.

"You could say that. Turkeys attacked me on the bike trail."

"That's terrible. I'll get you to the hospital." Sam helped him get his bike into the trunk.

"That won't be necessary. I'm just bleeding here and there. I'll patch up with some bandages."

"Where did this happen? And what's your name?"

"Jeff Smalley. I was on the Rock Island trail, south of Wyoming, headed north toward Tulon. I couldn't believe it at first, but as I saw more and more of them, and they pecked more and more chunks out of me, I turned around and headed back to Princeville. That's when you saw me."

"How long did they chase you?"

"Not long, only a quarter mile, but they were fast! I got up to twenty-five, and they were keeping up with me. Maybe I should take one or two along when I race. They really motivate you!"

"Did anyone else see the turkeys?"

"I saw no one on the trail."

"Count yourself lucky. These turkeys are killers."

"Yeah, I live in Princeville. I saw what they did there. I thought they had gone for good."

Sam drove Jeff to his home in Princeville. After making sure that Jeff was patched up, and giving him his business card, Sam drove up to Wyoming and asked about the zombie turkeys. No one in Wyoming had seen any. The zombie turkeys seemed to be lying low, despite their lack of strategy or intelligence. He stayed in Wyoming for the night. While driving around, Sam had seen the local TV vans and quite a few traffic copters as well as military copters and planes searching for the zombies and covering the story.

He wrote his story about the governor's press conference—using quotes Lisa provided—and his biker interview and emailed it to Lisa. Pretty thin pickings. The day seemed unexciting after the frantic battles the day before. He chuckled to himself. He was turning into an adrenaline junkie, looking for zombie turkey thrills each day.

* * *

He felt great. There was a lot of cover and forage for his flock. The predators were getting harder to kill, so he avoided them. He led his flock through the night along the rivers and creeks. When the woods ended, they crossed the fields in the dark to the nearest copse of trees. He caught a whiff of turkeys once again, upon the easterly wind. The flock immediately headed en masse toward Tom's Turkeys. In the predawn darkness, the turkeys could not be seen against the black earthen fields of November.

And they were outside the cordon, so no military patrols in the air or on the ground viewed them.

* * *

Tom's first turkey trap awoke him 5:00 a.m. with a roar. Tom had cleared out his woodshed and rigged it as a trap. Inside it, he penned some turkeys in a cage, thinking they would attract the zombie turkeys. If any zombie turkey entered, a photocell at the door triggered three chainsaws to start electrically and begin swinging back and forth from the ceiling. The chainsaws alone roared loudly, but the sounds of hundreds and thousands of turkeys screaming "Gobble! Gobble!" drowned out the three chainsaws. His blood ran cold. *That's a lot of turkeys.* He might need to use his apocalypse trap.

He turned on all the floodlights in the yard and saw that the traps he had at the doors to his barn had already been activated. These traps killed more gruesomely than the chainsaw one, but they weren't as noisy. These traps were a series of wooden boxes, three feet on a side. A turkey-sized hole, led to a turkey-sized tunnel, led to a turkey-sized trap door, led to a wood chipper. The chopped turkey went from the wood chipper into a bin.

Tom had joked to his wife he could sell this as turkey sausage.

He donned his beekeeper suit, which he had reinforced with duct tape and sheet metal, and walked out to the barn. Dozens of turkeys attacked him, but he swung his double-bladed axe and chopped up his share of turkeys. He made sure he split them in half, per the Princeville video instructions. With his double-bladed axe, he felt a little like Paul Bunyan.

Tom stomped into the barn through a sally door. He checked the back of each trap. He was glad he had borrowed the additional wood chipper from his brother-in-law. Ominously, ground turkey filled both sheet-metal bins almost completely. He imagined the traps getting clogged in a few more minutes. Time for the apocalypse trap.

He hadn't really intended to use this trap, because it was so dangerous. This was his *if everything goes to hell* plan. The ten thousand or more crazed, red-eyed turkeys attacking his turkey farm were not deterred by turkey blood or the noise of the chainsaws or the wood chippers. Their numbers would soon overwhelm his defenses. This trap had taken the most time to set up with his brother-in-law. He had tested the circuitry but not actually tested the trap. He hoped it worked.

Tom pulled the big knife-edged switch in his barn. KA-CHUNK! The lights in the yard and barn dimmed. All around the barn, servomotors whirred as long doors in the ground opened up, revealing trenches surrounding the barn. Thousands of turkeys dropped into the trenches. A few seconds later, the electric sparks activated, igniting the foot-deep gasoline in the trenches. Tom had used watering troughs and wood frames lined with plastic to hold the gasoline. Flames shot up to the top of the barn, drowning out the frantic "Gobble! Gobble!" noise.

Tom had intense satisfaction seeing thousands of turkeys scatter from his barn in every direction. He'd done it! He'd defeated the zombie turkeys! He took off the uncomfortable beekeeper helmet.

"Gobble! Gobble!" came from behind him.

Tom turned just in time to have his face gashed by a tom turkey spur. He grabbed his axe and swung, chopping the turkey's head off. Spurting blood, it walked and hopped aimlessly. He was about to chop it in half when he again heard "Gobble! Gobble!"

Another tom turkey—but this one was white, one of his own, but with the zombie-plague red eyes. Behind it loomed a crowd of white turkeys, all with blood-red eyes.

"Gobble! Gobble!"

Quickly, he grabbed his beekeeper helmet. Before he could put it on, zombie turkeys slashed his head and face a dozen times—Tom's farm turkeys. One cut severed his carotid artery. Even as he put his helmet on, Tom grew faint and fell into a pool of his own blood, mixed with that of the zombie turkeys. His pain soon ended.

"Gobble! Gobble!" The turkeys crowded around the body and tried to feed. The beekeeper suit frustrated them. They could only drink from the widening pool of blood.

* * *

He felt great. Full of energy. He had no memory of losing his head or of flying up to the top of the barn and into an open sky light. All he knew was he was happy to have thousands of new hens with which to breed. The massed turkeys broke down the door, flew out the skylights, and burst the screens. By dawn, the turkeys had gone out and into the cover of the woods.

* * *

A screaming, hysterical woman on the phone assailed the ear of Susan Byre, police dispatcher in Henry, Illinois. Eventually, she calmed enough to say her husband had been killed by turkeys, despite zombie turkey traps he had created. Twenty thousand new turkeys had been zombified from Tom's turkey farm.

Uh-oh. Twenty thousand plus ten thousand turkeys already out there equaled thirty thousand turkeys outside the National Guard cordon. And now the zombie turkeys had escaped into the Illinois River valley, full of parks and nature preserves. Susan immediately called the National Guard.

* * *

37

Early that same morning, General Bagley said bitterly to his National Guard staff officers, "We're in deep crap. The turkeys escaped our cordon and are into the Illinois River valley. Also, their numbers have tripled to thirty thousand. Our immediate objective is to keep them in the valley and not let them go up- or downriver. How do you propose to do that, given that they escaped you in wide-open, bare fields?" General Bagley's steely gray eyes bored into each of his officers in the room at Illinois National Guard headquarters. The turkeys' escape embarrassed him, and he wanted to take it out on his subordinates.

The general's top intelligence officer, Colonel Figeroa, replied, "We think they slipped under Route 40 through a culvert. They're using creeks and rivers as their roads, so we will watch all creeks and rivers going to and from the Illinois River south of Henry and north to Hennepin. We will contain them in this smaller area with more troops, more drones, and more night-vision goggles."

The colonel's cool blue eyes looked calmly into the general's angry ones.

"What about killing the buggers?" He shot out the words like bullets from a machine gun.

"It's pretty well established you've got to shred them, or at least cut them in half, to kill them. We're bringing up our new shoulder-mounted fléchette rockets. They launch from our hand-held rocket launchers. A standard round splits into a hundred fléchettes. They'll have enough power to go through a dozen turkeys. These rocket launchers are also semiautomatic. Each soldier's launcher has a five-shell magazine and can carry five of them. We have the same weaponry on our AH-64 Apache helicopters."

"How many soldiers and how many helicopters?"

"We have twenty-five hundred soldiers on foot and another five thousand supporting them. We have three squadrons of ten helicopters for three shifts of surveillance. All three squadrons can be activated at any time for any attacks on the turkeys."

Bagley grunted. "Should do. Don't screw up."

Early that same morning, Sam Melvin heard the police reports of the attack on Tom's Turkeys north of Henry. "That's outside the National Guard cordon," he said to himself. Heading for Henry along Route 17, he stopped alongside the road and tried to figure out how the turkeys did it. "Last known sighting along the Wyoming bike trail. Following that north, we've got several rivers and creeks. If they take the creeks, they can cross Route 40 here, near Lombardville, Illinois." They also could have crossed south near Bradford. He drew a dotted line of their likely route to Henry, wrote the speculative story, and sent it to Lisa for publication. He then drove north along 40 to the creek they might have followed. The creek at Bradford just ended in a cornfield. There were no signs of zombie turkeys having been there. Further north he hit pay dirt. He saw a National Guard truck and a squad of troops at the bridge over the creek. The creek wasn't much more than a yard wide: Fox Creek.

"Hello, men," he greeted the guardsmen. "See any signs of the turkeys?"

An amazingly young guardsman glanced deferentially at an older officer. "I'm Lieutenant Maxwell," said the middle-aged officer. "May I ask who you are, sir?"

"Sure. Sam Melvin, investigative reporter for the *Midley Beacon*. I think this is a likely spot for the turkeys to have gotten through your cordon last night, and I wanted to see if there were any signs of turkeys along this creek."

"You don't have to look. We've confirmed this is where they came through. They went under the road and through the culvert, while our infrared sensors and drones were looking up and down Route 40. General Bagley will have a press conference in Henry this afternoon." The officer spoke with rueful honesty.

"Thank you, Lieutenant Maxwell," Sam said. "I don't suppose there's any security about this information? It's not like turkeys are intelligent or anything," he said, quoting General Bagley.

"They may not be, but sometimes I wonder if we are. Don't quote me on that!" he added hurriedly, a touch of anxiety in his voice.

"Of course not. Good luck with your turkey hunting!"

In Henry, a small town of about two thousand, Sam asked if anyone else had been attacked or even seen the turkeys. He stopped at gas stations, quick marts, fast-food restaurants. No one had seen any turkeys. Sam also got directions to Tom's Turkeys. At Tom's turkey farm he had to deal with another grieving zombie turkey widow.

Knocking on the front door, he introduced himself. "Sam Melvin, investigative reporter from the *Midley Beacon*. Mrs. Tuffield, I can understand if you're not up to speaking right now. If you can, can you tell me your experiences today?"

Mrs. Tuffield, a sturdy brunette, was younger than Mrs. Yoder. Her dark eyes had circles under them, and her red eyes showed she had been crying.

She set her mouth in a firm, straight line and said, "You're the first reporter here, and I'll have to tell the story anyway, so it might as well be you. You're Sam Melvin? You're a celebrity! You're the one who posted those YouTube videos from Princeville. Tom watched them over and over and made his turkey traps. My name's Betty, by the way."

She led him from the front porch to a woodshed with a torn-off door.

Sam said, "Wow. I don't know what is more amazing: that I'm a celebrity or that someone paid so much attention to those videos!"

"Tom sure did. He started working on them the night after the Princeville attack. Here's the chainsaw one."

Sam glanced inside and saw a turkey abattoir. He estimated dozens of turkeys had been sawn to pieces in the woodshed. He took pictures and a video of the trap. "I'll write, 'Tom Tuffield took the zombie turkeys to the woodshed' in my story, Mrs. Tuffield."

"That's nothing," she sniffed. "Let me show you the turkey choppers."

She led him to the barn and past the now familiar zombie turkey–sprung door into the barn. A box with a three-foot-by-three-foot hole in it blocked the main door of the barn. Runnels of blood ran from it, forming a grisly, red puddle in front. In the barn rested the business end of the trap: a wood chipper and a bin overflowing with ground turkey.

"The other trap at the other door looks the same. Tom always liked cutting and splitting logs. He didn't need to for the farm. He just liked it to supply our woodstove," Betty said. She stopped, struck. "I guess he won't be chopping any more wood. I wonder who will do that for me?" Taking hold of herself with a sniff, she walked on.

A four-foot sheet-metal cube formed the bin of turkey sausage. Sam thought at least two hundred turkeys went into each of the bins. "I figure Tom's traps killed at least five hundred turkeys," he remarked.

"It's more like two or three thousand. Let me show you the apocalypse trap."

She led him to a blackened trench all around the rest of the turkey barn. Thousands of black lumps filled the trenches. "Tom filled those trenches with gasoline and then ignited them remotely from the barn. They were his last-ditch defense if the wood chippers failed. When those babies went up, the whole farm lit up like day."

Sam looked at the black smoke marks on the white sides of the metal barn

Betty sighed. "I expected to find Tom safe and sound in the office in his beekeeper suit. Instead, thousands of zombie turkeys, *our* turkeys, were pouring out of the barn. After they were gone, I found poor Tom." She started sobbing.

"I'm very sorry for your loss. You're the second turkey-farm widow I've met. You don't have to tell me any more."

"No, let me finish this. Perhaps someone else can benefit. I explored the barn and found the turkeys had flown up to the roof and gotten in an open skylight. The zombie infection must have spread like wildfire."

"Like the plague," murmured Sam. "Do you mind if I tell people about your zombie traps?"

She smiled grimly, "Not at all. My brother Jerry helped Tom make them. Put them on your website, and we'll sell them to other turkey farms in Illinois—along with our sausage. Tom joked about selling turkey sausage. Maybe I'll really do that. It'd be like a way of getting even."

"I've sure that won't be FDA allowable."

"I know that. I'll sell it as genuine zombie turkey sausage, not suitable for human consumption. A novelty item, like canned unicorn."

"Hmmm. You can advertise on the *Midley Beacon* YouTube site for free, if we get half the profits."

"That's too high. Make it a quarter, and you've got a deal. A widow's got to live." They shook on it.

* * *

"Hi, Lisa," Sam said on their daily call that evening.

"Hi, Sam. You've delivered another dynamite story today! You scooped the national media. They descended on Tom's turkey farm hours after you were there, and the widow—"

"Betty Tuffield."

"Of course. She referred them to our paper and our website. Sam, we're not only successful and famous, we're rich! Oprah contacted me today to have us on her show."

"Wow."

"Our YouTube videos have over thirty million hits. We're going up ten million hits a day! Oddly, we're most popular in Albania. We've added the Tuffield turkey traps and the Tuffield Genuine Zombie Turkey Sausage ads to our site."

"Betty called me before I called you. She got her brother to start making the traps immediately. She has over a thousand orders at a hundred percent markup. She also says the sausages are selling like hotcakes already. She got the turkey-farm helpers making them and boxing them. She's shipping them around the world in Styrofoam and dry ice." He chuckled. "That's really getting a business going at internet speed. She's already getting money through PayPal— that's before Tom's life insurance or flock insurance pays."

"What's our portion of the profit?"

"She's selling the sausages for ten dollars a pound. There's two dollars of cost for packing each and eight dollars of profit. We get two dollars a sausage."

"Wow. You've got me talking like you! How many pounds does she have?"

"Betty had about eight thousand pounds of raw turkey. She adds filler to each sausage. Plus, she also adds the burnt turkey carcasses. She'll get about twenty-five thousand sausages from that. That'll be fifty thousand bucks for us."

"The power of the internet. That's still small potatoes compared to the hundreds of thousands of dollars we're getting from news media around the world and ads on our YouTube site. Even our fifty thousand daily newspaper sales are small. Say, what's our portion of the profit on the turkey traps?"

"Uh, um, we didn't discuss that."

"That shyster! When Betty called me, she said you'd agreed to free advertising for a quarter of the profits! She emailed me ads for both the sausage and the turkey traps. I assumed she meant a quarter of the profits of each!"

"Calm down, Lisa. You just said this is small potatoes— small sausages—compared to the other income we have. Can't you give a grieving widow a break?"

Lisa sighed. "OK. But I've *got* to teach you how to negotiate in the future." After regaining her composure, Lisa continued, "Back to the news business. What's next for the zombie turkey flock, O my favorite zombie turkey whisperer?"

Lisa actually sounded friendly! He was so used to her prickly personality that her niceness flummoxed him. He was supposed to be the nice one. Uncertainly, he began, "I attended the news conference in Henry today. The military is going to try to contain the turkeys to this section of the Illinois River north of Henry and south of Spring Valley. They seemed grim and determined."

"Hmmph," she snorted. "They slipped away once. They'll slip away again."

"I'm not so sure. I can see half a dozen helicopters going up and down the river from here, and I'm sure there are more."

"Want to bet on it?"

"Sure. For what?"

"A nice dinner at the restaurant of the winner's choice. Loser pays. We both can afford it. Have you looked at your bank account lately?"

"Um, no."

"I had a ten-thousand-dollar bonus deposited there. That's on top of your new one-hundred-thousand-dollar salary."

"That's too much!"

"Don't sweat it. I'm making more. We're up to five employees now, besides us, the founders: one webmaster, an assistant editor, a full-time secretary, a full-time email person, and a full time printer. I just bought out the printer we've used for years, and he's devoting his whole time to our paper. Did you know people are subscribing to it from around the world? Not just our news website, but the paper version as well. Albania has over a thousand subscribers!"

"I can't believe it. Midley is on the map."

"Thanks to you, Sam. You've really achieved your potential."

"I think I was just lucky."

"No, you've always worked hard. I've always appreciated that. Your hard work met a great opportunity, and we can cash in."

"Lisa, I've known you since high school, but I never knew you thought this way."

"That's another thing. I get frustrated and impatient, and I take it out on you, and you never complain."

"Wow. I don't know what to say."

"Don't worry. I do. Get a good night's sleep, and hit the road early tomorrow morning."

"Good night, Lisa."

"Good night, Sam."

Chapter 5

Tiskilwa

Fletcher Axel had read of the zombie turkey advance with great concern. His farm sat just west of the cordon and east of Tiskilwa, a small village of eight hundred south of I-80. Fletcher raised organic, free-range turkeys. He could sell those for double the price of regular turkeys, and with Thanksgiving coming up, his sales were climbing. He did not have nearly the quantity the other turkey farmers had, only about five hundred or so, but he didn't want any to go zombie on him. He double-checked his barn—nice and tight all around, and he had wooden shutters on the windows and skylights. He made sure they were all latched—he had learned from Tom's Turkeys the day before. Thank God for the *Midley Beacon*!

Then his flamethrower came in the mail from Amazon—shipped for free. Now he felt comfortable he could hold the threat off. Even zombie turkeys feared fire. He looked up how to make napalm on the internet and made a fifty-five-gallon barrel of it. He ran a hose from it to his flamethrower and tested it behind the barn, using an old electric sump pump to propel the napalm. Quite satisfactory. He didn't need to worry his wife, Julie, about this, so he didn't tell her about his flamethrower.

He had always been an early riser, but since the zombie turkey threat arose, he'd been getting up by 3:00 a.m., getting his work done, and then going out and patrolling his fields in his John Deere tractor. He had an idea of how to use that as a weapon too. He carefully inspected the fences and woodlands to the east of the farm, adjoining the Illinois River valley, where the turkeys had last been seen.

His vigilance paid off three days later. At 6:30 a.m., he saw a group of turkeys coming from the east. He would have taken it as a normal flock of wild turkeys, which lived in the woods around the farm, but over half of them were pure white—domestic, farm-raised turkeys. He knew what that meant: zombie turkeys!

He drove at top speed across his fallow field to the equipment barn. He attached his forty-five-foot harrow and returned to the turkeys advancing his way. The flock had grown to hundreds. He drove into their midst. Plenty flew up, but a lot were slow on the switch, and the angled disks of the harrow cut the zombies into sliced turkey. He turned around and headed for the next big clump of them. Same result. After a dozen times across the field and hundreds of turkeys ground into fertilizer, the live turkeys started avoiding his tractor. He drove back to his turkey barn.

Several hundred turkeys crowded there, trying to get in and flying up to the roof. He climbed out of the tractor cab and fetched his flamethrower out of the shed. The hundred-foot-garden hose he'd used to link the flamethrower and the drum of napalm unwound from its reel next to the barrel of napalm. As soon as he walked out, the turkeys made a beeline for him—or was it a turkey line?

Grabbing the flamethrower, he turned on the pump and opened up. Turkey fricassee. He kept his back to his metal barn and slowly walked all the way around, flaming as he went. By the time he was three quarters of the way around, the turkeys had beat it—except for a couple hundred charred carcasses.

"Fletch! Yer goin' to kill yerself!" his wife yelled.

"Mebbe so, but at least the turkeys won't."

"Was that those zombie turkeys?"

"Sure was. Red eyes and all, just like they said in the paper. They're daid now."

"You'd better let that fellar Sam Melvin know."

"Now, how would I get ahold of him?"

"He put a phone number on his website for Hot Turkey Tips."

"These sure are hot turkeys all right." After a last survey around the barnyard, he clambered back into the tractor and double-checked the field. Sure enough, a few stragglers rose from the ground, so bloody and dirty he couldn't tell if they if they were domestic or wild. He harrowed them under. Then he called Sam Melvin.

* * *

"Hello, Sam Melvin, investigative reporter for the *Midley Beacon*," Sam said. He was already on the road, his trusty Roadwarrior Bluetooth headset serving him as he drove toward Spring Valley. He had spent the night in Henry.

"*The* Sam Melvin?"

"Yes, that's me."

"Ya answer your own Turkey Hot Line?"

"Sure. I know the most about these turkeys. Do you have a turkey sighting?"

"You betcha—about two thousand of 'em."

"What? Where?"

"Right at my farm west of Tiskilwa."

"That's the opposite direction of what I expected! Who is this anyway?"

"Fletcher Axel. I grow organic free-range turkeys."

"Is anyone hurt there?"

"Yup. About a thousand very dead turkeys."

"No resurrections?"

"A few got back up after I harrowed 'em. I harrowed 'em again."

"Fantastic! I'll be right there. What's your address?"

"Rural Route 17, Tiskilwa Bottom Road."

After an extralegal U-turn, Sam exceeded the posted fifty-five-miles-per-hour speed limit, but not the seventy-miles-per-hour highway limit, to Tiskilwa Bottom Road, so he thought he was good.

The rising smoke on the horizon showed him the location of Fletcher's farm. The turkey carcasses still smoldered on the ground. "Talk about a hot lead," he muttered to himself. He parked in the drive, and a buxom blonde met him at the door.

What a hot woman, Sam thought.

"Hi, Sam! I'm Julie Axel. Can I get yer autograph?"

"Um, yes." He signed her high school yearbook. *Best regards to Julie. Sam Melvin.* It was the first time anyone had asked for his autograph. Even in his own high school no one had signed his yearbook or asked him to sign theirs.

"Couldja post a video of us tellin' the turkey battle?"

"Sure. Let's get started."

Sam videoed Fletcher on this tractor running his harrow, the turkey pieces remaining in the field, Fletcher's flamethrower, and his fifty-five gallon drum of napalm, now down to about fifteen gallons. He closed with Fletcher demonstrating his flamethrower on the charred turkey carcasses.

"Do ya wanna video me makin' napalm?" Fletcher asked as they walked back to the house.

"No, there are already tons of videos about that. Let's stick to the story. I've got another question."

"Shoot."

"Your turkey farm wasn't listed when I searched the internet for Illinois turkey farms."

"Yeah, I try to stay off the grid and under the radar. I only access the internet using anonymizing servers and incognito browsers."

"How did you buy the flamethrower on Amazon?"

"I used my wife's credit card."

"OK. Do you know of any other small turkey farmers around here? They're all vulnerable."

"Yeah, but they're not vulnerable. They're all survivalists, like I am. There's a group of us free-range turkey farmers here in Illinois. I really can't give out their names."

"Can we at least call the nearest ones and make sure they're OK?"

"Sure. I'll activate our emergency phone-calling tree and alert them."

"You have an organic-turkey-farmer-and-survivalist calling tree?"

"Sure. Ya'll never know when the apocalypse hits. Maybe this is it!"

"Do you mind if I call the National Guard?"

"Nah. I support our military."

From the Axels' kitchen, Sam called Lisa, whom he knew had contacts in the Illinois National Guard.

"Hi, Lisa, I need your help."

"What's up, Sam?"

"I'm here at Fletcher Axel's turkey farm. He had a turkey attack, and he managed to defeat them!"

"Wow! There I go again—you're a bad influence! Get me that story, ASAP!"

"Sure thing. About that help I need: I know you have contacts in the National Guard. Tip them off about this attack. They need to know."

"Sure, Sam. Be sure to send that story with the videos! The *Midley Beacon* profit engine needs to be stoked!"

Sam had just finished a ham-and-egg breakfast from Julie and posted his story and videos, when an AH-64 Apache landed in the field. All three of them ran out to greet the pilot and his passenger.

"Hello, folks. I'm Lieutenant Robert Maxwell. Hi, Sam. Long time no see."

"Hello, Lieutenant."

"You guys know each other?" Julie said in awe.

"We just met the other day," Sam explained.

"We saw the smoke from the farm and came in to investigate."

Fletcher, his wife, and Sam related the battle. Sam videoed the helicopter.

"Well done. You seem really well prepared, Mr. Axel," Lieutenant Maxwell said.

"Thanks. That means a lot, coming from one of our nation's military."

They'd just finished briefing the intelligence officer, when a V-22 Osprey landed.

Technical specialists spilled out, taking pictures and gathering up turkey carcasses.

The intelligence officer said to Sam, "You folks from the *Midley Beacon* have been a great help, Sam. We in the military thank you for your detailed reporting. We have used it—just don't tell anyone." A crackling radio interrupted him. "Code red! Turkey attack reported west of Bureau Junction." Immediately the lieutenant and all the specialists ran to the helicopter and Osprey and took off.

"Crap," Fletcher said. "Bureau Junction's where my friend Vern lives. He has an organic turkey farm too. I hope he got the warning phone call in time."

* * *

Vern Wilcox had gotten the phone call in time. In late middle age, he was pushing sixty, and he had the gray hair to prove it. As a survivalist, he was well prepared with automatic weapons, an underground bunker stocked with food, and a variety of explosives. He had shooed his family into the bunker and had just climbed to the M2 .50 caliber machine gun nest in his barn rooftop, when he saw the wave of zombie turkeys coming at his barn across the field. He had gotten the machine gun from his dad, who had brought it home after WW II. He had over ten thousand rounds for it, enough for twenty-five minutes of continuous fire. Even with thousands of turkeys charging him, he couldn't fire continuously; the barrel would melt down. He also had a change of barrels, which he knew from practice was absolutely necessary.

He had the ammo wound on a spool he scavenged from a cable TV company. That way, he didn't need another person to feed the ammo. He had an electric motor that turned the spool when the belt tension reached a critical point. The .50 caliber belts had to be fed carefully to prevent jamming. He opened fire while the zombie turkeys were four hundred yards away. He heard their banshee cries echoing across the field.

"Gobble! Gobble!"

They went down just like a field of wheat in a hailstorm. A single shell would go through half a dozen turkeys, and he felled hundreds upon hundreds. The turkey flood petered out to a trickle of a couple dozen scattered individuals.

His gun jammed.

"Crap," he commented. "At least it lasted long enough to break their attack." Then the mangled turkeys started to rise and stagger toward his barn.

"Gobble! Gobble!"

He hurriedly changed the barrel. The gun was still jammed. He started taking apart the breach and then realized *all* the turkeys he had shot were up walking and almost at the barn.

"I got just the thing for you guys." He picked up his M82 .50 caliber sniper gun and mounted a grenade on it. BLAM! A ten-foot hole opened in the wave of turkeys. BLAM! BLAM! BLAM! BLAM! BLAM! BLAM! BLAM! BLAM! BLAM! BLAM! BLAM! Twelve holes opened up. A thousand turkeys were blown to red mist. Another thousand surrounded his barn. He was out of grenades, and with a jammed gun. The turkeys couldn't get through the sheet-metal barn and doors, but they were flying up to him. They were still bloody shreds, but they bounded closer and closer. Each time they hopped and flew up, they were a little less bloody, a little less mangled, with a little more feathers, and flew a little higher, closer and closer to his machine gun nest on top of his barn.

Vern took out his M11 .45 caliber pistol. That would be a little handier at close range than his M82 if they came in the top of the barn. "I'll go down shooting," he vowed. He continued to work on clearing the jam in his machine gun.

Then the marines landed in a V-22 Osprey. One of their observation drones had seen the turkey attack and notified National Guard headquarters. They dispatched the Osprey and Apache. The Apache shot fléchette rockets from the sky. The turkeys turned into shredded meat. The marines slid down, rappelling lines from the Osprey, and formed two firing squads. They had shoulder-mounted versions of the same fléchette weapon and shot enfilading fire along two different diagonals. The mass of attacking turkeys were now turkey burgers.

"Thanks, guys. You saved my butt," Vern said as he approached the marines.

"Anyone else around here?" the helmeted marine lieutenant asked.

"My family's in our bunker."

"You had some heavy weaponry here, but it wasn't suited for zombie turkey attacks. You need to shred them, or at least cut them in half. Did they get into your turkey barn?"

"Nope."

"You'd better check."

Vern was miffed the lieutenant criticized his weaponry. *Snotty lieutenant*, he thought. He was as well prepared as anyone. Right then Vern decided to get a flamethrower, like his buddy Fletcher had. Vern had five hundred thirty-four turkeys, and they were all clean and black eyed, like turkeys should be.

Sam and Fletcher showed up soon afterward. Julie came in another car with her kids. Sam recorded the victory on video and interviewed Lieutenant Maxwell describing it.

Afterward, Sam commented to Vern, "Wow. You've got some amazing weaponry here."

"Thanks," Vern said proudly. "I got it surplus, and I've practiced with it for years."

"Is everyone in your organic turkey association armed like you are?"

"Pretty much. I have more than most. Now Fletcher, he's the only one who got a flamethrower. I think a lot of us are going to get flamethrowers now."

Vern's wife, Ethel, offered to cook breakfast for the bunch of them. Sam said, "This'll be the second breakfast for me, ma'am, but I'll take it. No telling when my next meal might come."

Before Sam left for Spring Valley, Lieutenant Maxwell advised, "General Bagley will have another press conference in Hennepin this afternoon. You might want to be there."

"Thanks," Sam said as he shook the lieutenant's hand. He bid farewell to Fletcher and Julie, Vern and Ethel, and their kids and left for Hennepin.

Chapter 6

Hennepin

That afternoon, after being introduced by the state public relations manager, Florence Gunderson, General Bagley opened the press conference in the village of Hennepin at the largest room in the Putnam County Courthouse. "Ladies and gentlemen, I'd like to introduce Dr. Edwin Galloway of the Poultry Research Institute in Northwestern University. He has the preliminary results of the studies on the turkey disease that has produced these 'zombie turkeys.'" He made quotation marks with his fingers. "Dr. Galloway."

A tall, slender man stepped to the microphone. He had dark-brown hair, a thin face, and glasses. "Thank you, General Bagley. When we received the turkey samples, we quickly identified the pathogen as a rapidly growing bacterial infection, spread pneumatically. That is, through the air and by breathing. It can also be spread by blood contact.

"The bacterium seems normal, but it mutates rapidly, depending upon the tissue in which it is found. It captures the local cell's DNA, and replicates it, and actually becomes that kind of cell very rapidly, within minutes. The net effect is that bacterium mimics the body tissue and avoids the body's immune-system response. Bacterially replicated tissue rapidly replaces damaged tissue. This causes the damaged turkey to regenerate, even from the brink of death—or beyond.

"By that, I mean fresh turkey carcasses can come back to life through this bacterium. Muscles, nerves, and organs regenerate within minutes. The heart starts beating, and you have a zombie turkey. We have replicated this in our laboratory with fresh turkeys bought from a local store.

"Furthermore, these bacterially produced tissues are stronger and more durable than normal turkey tissues. You end up with stronger and tougher turkeys. The more the turkeys are injured and their wounds regenerate, the stronger they become.

"This disease is fascinating medically, but from a public health point of view, we want to stop it. We've found a simple and effective technique: salt water. Salt water injected into turkeys completely eliminates the disease and reverses its effect. Back to you, General Bagley."

"Thank you, Dr. Galloway, for you and your team's quick and effective research on this disease. This morning we used our new shoulder-mounted fléchette weapon to good effect at an attack on a turkey farm west of Hennepin. We are currently modifying the fléchette weapon to inject salt water into the turkeys. Each fléchette will be replaced by a syringe with salt water. A single dose will dezombify a turkey," General Bagley spoke confidently to the assembled reporters.

"This threat is by no means eliminated yet. We have successfully contained the turkeys to the Illinois valley area, but given the fact the infection is passed pneumatically, every turkey farm in Illinois is vulnerable. We cannot contain bacteria. We will visit each turkey farm and help them guard against outbreaks.

"That's our latest news for you. The floor is now open for questions."

"Dr Galloway, can we develop a vaccine for this disease?" asked Gail Caltrop from CNN.

"Vaccines are for viral infections, not bacterial. The turkey farmers will need to guard against infections with a daily salt water spray, until we develop an effective antibiotic."

"General Bagley, do you have a list of the turkey farms in Illinois?" asked Sam Melvin of the *Midley Beacon*.

"We have a list of fifteen large and small ones. However, there are many small, undocumented farms which are not publically listed. We are appealing to the public to help us find these farms and protect them from this plague."

"Dr. Galloway, isn't the Poultry Research Institute in Northwestern University also popularly known as the 'Turkey Institute'?" queried Bonnie Blatt of the *Normal Shout*.

He smiled and chuckled. "Yes, we started calling it that among ourselves because turkeys and chickens dominate our work. My own doctoral research was on cloning turkeys. However, the official name is the 'Poultry Research Institute in Northwestern University.'"

Sam took notes throughout the conference. He'd have to pry the list of organic turkey farmers away from Fletcher Axel as soon as he could. He doubted Fletcher knew the danger his organic turkey group faced from the air-borne contagion or how to protect their turkeys from it.

Aside from reporting on the press conference, Sam also covered the public reaction to the zombie turkey plague. The towns of Spring Bay, Hennepin, and Henry had closed schools and organized public-defense militia against the ravaging flocks of zombies. There had already been small attacks outside of Hennepin fended off by groups with shotguns and flamethrowers.

After the conference, Sam wrote in his hotel room, over the pizza he had delivered. He had to finish the last story before he collapsed. Getting up at 4:00 a.m. played havoc with his sleep schedule, but that schedule worked for him. The turkeys usually attacked at dawn, and he'd been on the scene more often than not. Once more, he looked at his map.

Sam placed a marker at each known turkey attack. After Tom's turkey farm, they had moved upstream to Hennepin. They had tried to burst out of the cordon to the west and had been defeated. They had been conquered in Bureau Junction and outside Hennepin. Sam thought they would flee to the east, along the river to Spring Valley. That was where he'd go tomorrow morning.

He had talked with Fletcher Axel, and while he hadn't given out any names, he had promised to call each of his friends in the organic-turkey organization and give them the urgent message about turkey sanitation.

The phone rang. It was Lisa.

"Hi, Sam."

"Hi, Lisa."

"No big news from me—it's all coming from you! You keep topping yourself. On our bet, so far you're winning."

"Oh, you mean on whether the turkeys would burst out of the military cordon?"

"Yes. I've got a nice French restaurant all planned out to take you. Let's give it four more days—that'll make it a week."

"That'll be great. I've had second thoughts though, and so has General Bagley. I think I'll still have to pay you, since the Turkey Institute's report indicated the infection can be spread through the air."

"Let's meet in four days no matter what, at the French restaurant. I miss you."

"Wow. Thanks, Lisa. I don't know what to say."

"You don't have to talk—you write so well. I'll do the talking."

"That's fine with me. Where is this place?"

"It's in Joliet. You're headed that way anyway."

"Let's hope we get there before the turkeys do."

"You're right. What are you using for turkey defense?"

"My big old Lincoln and a heavy foot."

"You idiot! I mean, once you're out."

"Hmm. Against a flock of turkeys, anything short of a flamethrower doesn't do much."

"So get one."

"A flamethrower!?!"

"Sure. You said Fletcher Axel bought one on Amazon."

"OK, let me look online while I have you on the phone. Oh, wow, there it is! Fifty-foot range, CO_2 powered. This is what Fletcher adapted for his defense."

"Order it! I don't feel you're safe without it! Send it by priority delivery. I just got an Amazon Prime account. The *Midley Beacon* will pay for it. Be sure to put it on your expense report."

"Done. Thanks for looking out for me. Just because I haven't been eaten yet by a zombie turkey doesn't mean my name isn't on the lips of the next zombie turkey."

"Snork!" she snorted. "Turkeys don't have lips."

"It's a zombie mutation."

"On that note, I'll say good night, Sam. See you in Joliet!"

Chapter 7

Joliet

He felt great. Full of energy. He had a big flock of hens and subservient toms. He vaguely recalled being shot and burned, but the past didn't bother him. He had to lead his flock.

Foraging had been good. Not only did they have many insects and frogs by the river and seeds in the forest to eat, but they'd been able to gobble several predators. They had gathered many wild turkeys and freed some of those white turkeys that had been imprisoned. They were all part of the flock now.

The predators had taken to attacking from the sky and fighting with fire. He avoided those areas and stayed under the trees. They hid during the day and came out at night, like now.

Most of the flock roosted by the riverside. A small, quiet island lay connected to the shore. He led his flock there. A series of islands dotted the river. The flock spread out over them. They found a few predators on the islands, which they quickly ate. Then the islands started to move.

The moving islands mildly surprised him, but felt safe; they couldn't be attacked while on the island, whether moving or not. The turkeys soon found the island had caves full of grain, on which they gorged. He waited for daylight by mating with his hens.

The majority of the flock joined him on the string of islands. A small portion paralleled them upstream along the river bank.

* * *

The guardsmen on cordon duty whispered to each other while they watched the riverside with night-vision goggles.

"Woah! Do you see that?"

"Yeah, thousands of turkeys coming through the woods toward us."

"I think we need reinforcements."

"Well, *duh*! Of course." Calling his sergeant, he said, "Sarge, we've got several thousand turkeys headed toward our position on the Illinois River. We won't be able to hold them off. Can you get some support for us?"

"I'll send up a squad of ten rocket launchers."

"When will they be here?"

"In fifteen minutes."

"The turkeys will be here in five."

"So hold them off for ten more minutes. You have fléchette launchers and flamethrowers with you."

"OK. But if we die due to turkeys, I'll come back from the dead and haunt you!"

"If you die due to turkeys, it'll be because you're a turkey. See you soon, Private Cowper. Sergeant Smith, out."

The fléchette launchers put holes in the turkey advance, but the flamethrowers really stopped them cold—or hot. The zombie turkeys gathered outside the circle of flames around the soldiers' position, their red eyes gleaming. The burnt turkeys in the napalm-fueled fire glowed like coals in hell.

Then the cavalry arrived—that was, the First Cavalry Division of the US Army, who had arrived in Joliet the previous day. Now they came west of Spring Valley in their Hummers and Bradley Fighting Vehicles. The Bradley's twenty-five-millimeter cannon opened up. A previously secret antipersonnel (in this case, antiturkey) round of four fléchettes in each twenty-five-millimeter round turned the massed turkeys into red mist. A few minutes later, dozens of soldiers piling out of the vehicles opened up with their shoulder-mounted fléchette rockets. Soon, the two thousand turkeys turned to red mud, flowing into the river.

"Men, fix bayonets, go through the turkeys' position, and look for survivors. If you find any, split them in two." Several dozen soldiers ran to do the gory task.

Sam Melvin reported on this victory the next morning, but the following couple of days were quiet. Too quiet. The citizens began discussing when to open the schools. The volunteer militia began complaining about the early morning patrols in the frosty dawn.

Not that there wasn't any news. Of the fifteen organic turkey farmers in the co-op Fletcher Axel belonged to, five had lost their flocks completely to the disease. The farmers and their families escaped death through vigorous application of ammunition and napalm. However, some farmers woke up one morning, and their turkeys were all gone. A total of five thousand turkeys joined the flock of zombie turkeys. Two other farms had some diseased turkeys, but the owners caught the disease in time and cured the turkeys with salt water.

Finally the day came for Sam's date with Lisa. It was funny. They had known each other since he was a sophomore in high school, and they had never dated. They'd worked together for fifteen years, and they never dated. The thought of dating her had occurred to him when he first met her—she was a looker, but she was a year older, and he'd never had the nerve. He was always shy around girls anyway. After they had worked well together at the school newspaper, when she'd started the *Midley Beacon*, she'd invited him to work with her again. The pay wasn't much, but then it didn't cost much to live in Midley. He'd gotten an apartment in town, then eventually he'd renovated an old house with his dad, which he now owned free and clear. He'd often thought he should leave for a bigger city and better pay, but then he'd see Lisa's scowl in the morning, and he'd want to stay.

What was with Lisa anyway? She always bristled at everything—sensitive, impatient, and quick to anger. Now this friendly, nice stuff threw him off balance. Where was all of this going?

He dressed in his one plaid sports coat and the tie he'd worn at his high school graduation, and hoped it would be good enough for her. It was a good thing he hadn't gained much weight since high school. That was how she affected him. He always wanted to do his best, but it was never good enough for her; she'd always find some fault. Now she was all sunshine and joy—what did she want of him? This was an unprecedented situation, sort of like the zombie turkey plague.

He was early, but Lisa already waited at the restaurant, Bon Appetite. Her smile lit up her face. "Sam! You look great! Have you ever been here before?"

"Can't say I have."

"It's the best place in Joliet. Wait until you taste their filet mignon."

The food tasted very good. Lisa picked a good wine, with their meal and the evening flew by. The dessert, crème brûlée, added just the right touch afterward. As they sipped their coffee, Lisa said, "You're probably wondering why I wanted this date."

"Well, yes. It's our first after seventeen years of knowing each other."

"Ha! You're right. Well, let me start at the beginning. In high school, I thought you were a drip, but then I thought all boys were clods. I wanted a storybook hero who would sweep me off my feet. Handsome, strong, and courageous, he would be my ideal. I was very immature.

"In the years of working with you, I've come to respect your work ethic and your diligence in getting the job done, no matter what. Also, you were very easy to work with—I never had to tell you anything twice. The respect I had for you has exploded since the zombie turkey story began."

"That's kind of a crazy metaphor: respect exploded into what?"

"I saw you as a very courageous reporter. You continually put yourself into danger for the sake of the paper and, I hope, for my sake."

"Well, yes. I did it for the paper. I did it for you—you *are* the paper."

"And your fabulous reporting that has made us both wealthy and famous, was that for me too?"

"Yes. I work harder when I have a goal, a purpose to my life. I don't really think about the danger, even though I've seen plenty of death from the zombie turkeys."

"Could I ever be your goal, your purpose?"

"Well, you kind of are already. I like working for you and with you. I've thought of leaving for another paper, but then I'd see you in the morning, and I'd put it off for another day."

"So even though you were underpaid—don't argue; I know you were; I paid you—you stayed in Midley because of me?"

"Well, yes."

"These zombie turkeys have changed my life. They've made me question what I'm living for, what I'm waiting for. As you said, my name might be on the lips of the next zombie turkey. You asked me what my respect exploded into. It exploded into—love. I love you, Sam Melvin."

Sam was stunned. If she had turned into a zombie, he wouldn't have been more surprised. He knew she kind of liked him, in her way, but love? *Him*? He had always been kind of a nothing guy. He had volunteered for the multimedia lab in school, but no athletics, no academics. Lisa had always been the brain.

"Furthermore—" She knelt down in front of him. "Sam Melvin, will you marry me? I ask, not afraid of being too forward, but knowing you're shy and you'd never do it."

"I...uh. Wow. Yes, I guess."

"'Yes, I guess?' Don't be too enthusiastic," she said with a hint of her normal sharp asperity. "I probably won't kill you through marriage."

He laughed. "Thanks for the reassurance! Yes, if you're willing to marry me, I'm more than willing to marry you!"

"Whee! I can't believe it!" Lisa jumped up and hugged him, sitting in his lap. "Waiter, let's have a bottle of Dom Pérignon. We've just gotten engaged. All thanks to the zombie turkeys," she added with a giggle.

They finished off the bottle, and then Lisa said, "Let's move this party to the car!" Sam, just drunk enough, agreed.

They drove to a little park by the Des Plaines River, where it came into Joliet. They began kissing. Sam had no experience, and neither did Lisa, so they fumbled their way through with laughter, teeth clicking together like castanets.

Then there came a tapping on the window. A giant, red-eyed tom turkey made a crack in their window.

"Gobble! Gobble!"

"Aiee!" they screamed. Thousands of turkeys surrounded them. Sam started the engine and shifted into reverse. He squished so many turkeys, the wheels started spinning. It was like being stuck in deep snow—or red mud. Hundreds of turkeys pecked at the windows.

"If only we had a flamethrower!" Lisa cried.

"We do! The flamethrower I ordered from Amazon is in the backseat. I just picked it up today!"

Lisa dove into the backseat. She had wanted to get Sam into the backseat with her, but this wasn't the way or the time. She climbed back into the front seat with the flamethrower and the tank of napalm.

"Hold on, Sam! Here goes!" Lisa cracked the window and thrust out the flamethrower nozzle. Turkeys jammed their heads into the crack immediately.

"Gobble! Gobble!"

She shot flame fifty feet from the car. Sam spun the car around in a circle of death. The spinning freed up the car from the turkey guts covering the ground.

"Eat flame and die, turkeys!" Lisa yelled.

Dozens of napalm-soaked turkeys burst into flame, like avian fireworks. The others may have had bird brains, crazed by the zombie bacterium, but they knew enough to get away. Just as suddenly as they appeared, the turkeys vanished. Once again, flames had driven them away.

"Is that what you've had to go through these past two weeks?"

"No, I've missed most of the actual battles. This was the worst experience I've had." *So far*, he thought. "We'd better call the National Guard. They've broken out of the cordon again. I guess I owe you for the dinner," he said with a smile.

"No." She smiled back. "It's a business expense for the paper. We were discussing a corporate merger. Be sure to put it on your trip report. I've got General Bagley's cell phone. He really likes your reporting and told me to call him if we hear of any outbreak. This is an outbreak worse than Ebola or Zika. Who knows how far they may spread?"

* * *

Fred Hildebrandt finished fishing the Des Plaines River for Asian carp that evening. He worked a day job hauling fertilizer and then supplemented his meager income by commercial fishing at night. Asian carp were highly popular among the Asian immigrants in the area. He needed the money for his wife and four kids—and one on the way.

Fred had just hauled in his last netful, spread his nets to dry, and headed home, when he passed a string of barges docked south of Joliet. The odd thing was, there was an incessant "Gobble! Gobble!" coming from the barges. It sounded like a turkey farm! Then turkeys flew from the barges and landed on his boat!

"Gobble! Gobble!"

One look at their red eyes and he realized these were the zombie turkeys he had heard so much about. He thought they had been sealed up downriver. And what were they doing on barges?

Before the turkeys could attack him, he grabbed his fishing nets and threw them over the dozen or so turkeys on his boat.

"Gobble! Gobble!" They pecked and kicked helplessly at the net.

He threw them off the boat. The weights on the nets took them to the bottom of the river. He hauled the nets back up. No turkeys. Meanwhile, more turkeys landed on his boat. He repeated the process, over and over, until he exhausted his already tired body. By then, the barges no longer rang of "Gobble! Gobble!" Nor did his boat. He smiled. Perhaps he had helped himself by feeding the zombies to the fishes. "Now you're sleeping with the fishes," he said aloud, in his best mobster imitation.

* * *

Herman and Hester McDonald were eating out with their friends Joel and Angie Fegan, in Joliet. As retirees, they socialized several times a week. As usual, they were discussing the zombie turkey attacks of the past week. *Discussing*, that was, in the sense of arguing. Herman said, "I tell you, this whole zombie turkey thing is greatly exaggerated. In fact, I think it is a hoax by the federal government to take over our country. This is just like the Feds secretly causing 9/11 to happen."

"You're a whack job, Herman," Herman's friend Joel said fondly. He'd called him much worse before. "If the Feds are using this to take over the country, they're doing it all wrong.

Thousands of people are arming themselves with shotguns and flamethrowers and chainsaws, gun laws be damned."

"Pleeease, do we have to go into this again? Can't we just enjoy our hamburgers and fries?" Hester begged.

"Don't whine, Hester. You know I can't stand that tone of voice," Herman whined.

"Gobble! Gobble!"

"Is that you again, Angie? I have to say, you've gotten better at your turkey imitations," Joel said. Ever since the zombie turkeys had dominated the news cycle, Angie had taken to imitating turkey calls to scare people.

"No, that wasn't me. It was outside. It was very good though." They looked outside at the parking lot, where several people pointed into the evening darkness. One man jumped hurriedly into his car and drove away, squealing his tires. Another person ran into the restaurant.

"Everyone go home! The zombie turkeys are coming! The zombie turkeys are coming!" Then he ran out to his car.

"Bull! This is just a practical joke, a prank. I won't fall for it!" Herman stated positively. Another car took off, peeling rubber.

"Hmm. Angie, maybe we'd better go, just in case." Joel left money on the table with their unfinished meal and left with Angie. They weren't exactly running, but they weren't dawdling either.

"Joel, Angie, you can't take this seriously!" Herman shouted at their retreating backs. "Chickens!"

Joel and Angie's car pulled away, and Hester said, "Herman, what if there is something to this? You don't want to be caught here, do you?"

"Bull! I said it before, and I say it again: Bull! I'm going to finish my meal. I paid for it. Eat yours, Hester."

As they ate, another man ran out of the restaurant to his car. As he got to it, a tidal wave of poultry overwhelmed him. He managed to open the car door and slam it shut. Several turkey butts hung out of the door.

"Gobble! Gobble!"

"Herman! There they are!"

"I'll be damned. The zombies are real, red eyes, carnivorous and all."

"Let's go to our car!"

"It'll be safer staying here. They can't get in the restaurant." Thousands of red-eyed turkeys surrounded the restaurant, pecking on the thick, glass windows.

"Gobble! Gobble!"

The man in the vehicle outside started his car, revved it, and put it in gear. The wrong gear. The car surged forward and through the window. The tough plate glass shattered into a flower of shards. The flower disappeared, leaving a bouquet of zombie turkeys flying into the restaurant.

"Gobble! Gobble!" Like a black tide of death, inexorably rising, they swarmed over those in the restaurant. The mounds of pecked victims surmounted, quivering for a while, and then were still.

* * *

Fifty-three people were bowling at the Bowl-Mor Lanes when the turkeys came. "Gobble! Gobble!" Nearly a thousand superstrength turkeys bowled their way through the glass doors, shattering it with iron-hard beaks and claws, and ran into the thirty lanes where cosmic bowling was underway. Glow sticks marked the lane returns and glowing bowling balls provided fitful, flickering light as the red-eyed zombies advanced. Most bowlers just stared at the onrushing mass of gobblers, too amazed to act. One was holding a beer when a tom flew up and put out his eyes. One hurled his ball at the attackers, smashing a few, before dozens of turkeys overwhelmed him.

"Gobble! Gobble!"

Everyone ran screaming then. However, turkeys could run up to twenty-five miles per hour. Only one person escaped.

The one escapee, teenager Liz Latrell, ran down the alley and into the ball return and pin-setting room.

* * *

Sam and Lisa found a girl dazed, bloody, and wandering the streets of Joliet in her torn clothes later that night, without a winter coat.

"Hi, can we help you?" Sam said to her after he had pulled up the car next to her.

"Uh, I'm cold."

"Come inside. It's dangerous wandering around with the zombie turkey flocks roaming about."

Sam glanced at Lisa. They couldn't interview the girl right now, dazed as she was. But he felt she had a story to tell.

Sam pulled up to an all-night Denny's restaurant. "Let's get you something warm to eat."

He bought her steak and eggs with hot coffee.

"My name's Sam Melvin. I'm a reporter for the *Midley Beacon*. This is my fiancée, Lisa Kambacher."

Lisa beamed at him.

"Um, thanks for the food, Mr. Melvin, Ms. Kambacher. I'm Liz Latrell," she said through a mouthful of food.

"Just call us Lisa and Sam. Are you getting warmer?" Lisa said.

"Yeah." She patted her pants and then began crying.

"What's the matter, dear?" Lisa asked.

"M-m-my cell phone is gone. I left it at the bowling alley, with my coat. I can't even call my parents!"

"You can borrow mine," Lisa said.

"Th-th-thanks," she said, sniffing. She dialed her parents'.

"Hi, Mom. Yeah, I'm OK. B-b-but the t-t-turkeys got all my friends!" She burst into tears again. Lisa hugged her.

"Tell your mom we'll take you home."

"Th-th-thanks, Ms. K—er, Lisa."

On their way to Liz's house, she told them of the attack on Bowl-Mor Lanes, running down the bowling lane and hiding in the pin-changing room until the turkeys were gone. Her high school bowling team had been practicing there when the turkeys hit. Everyone in the alley had been killed but her. Stunned by the violent death of her friends, Liz wandered in the freezing-cold night until Sam and Lisa found her.

Lisa comforted her in the backseat while Sam drove.

"Liz, we'll go to Bowl-Mor and get your jacket and your phone."

"OK. Thanks, Mr.—Sam. It was lane twenty-four."

Her story dovetailed with his and Lisa's and hundreds of other people who had been attacked while going about their business last night in Joliet. What had kept the deaths under a thousand was that the attacks took place after 7:00 p.m., and most people were at home. However, Joliet lay outside the National Guard cordon, and no militia had been organized, nor had the children been kept home from school—until the day after the attack.

People who were attacked in restaurants, nightclubs, supermarkets, big-box stores, and other all-night locales had fled in panic. One man told Sam of being carjacked by a crazed couple using steak knives from the local restaurant. He had driven them away from the tsunami of zombie turkeys to their home outside of Joliet. They then apologized for the hijacking and paid for his gas.

Along the same lines, the Joliet police reported dozens of parked cars had been stolen from around the Des Plaines River, from where the turkeys had attacked. In desperation to get away, many people had hotwired the cars and later abandoned them.

The Farm Fresh Turkey Farm south of Joliet had the worst news, however. It had been attacked first, and the turkeys caught the owners totally unprepared. Now they were totally dead. Over seventy thousand turkeys in ten different barns had escaped and presumably followed the zombie turkey flock into Joliet.

Lisa stayed with Sam all through the night as they went from place to place, tracking the zombie turkey attacks. They used their flamethrower once more, but this time they were on offense. The zombie turkeys were attacking a car wash when the couple heard the eerie "Gobble! Gobble" cries. The employees were helpless, trapped in the car wash while zombie turkeys flooded in the two entrances. A touch of napalm at the entrances sent hundreds of turkeys scattering, while leaving dozens of burning zombie turkey bodies.

Governor Brooks and President Obama declared Joliet a disaster area. The next morning, FEMA, the Federal Emergency Management Agency, arrived in Joliet. There were over a thousand victims, tens of thousands grieving family members, and property damage. FEMA workers established health aid stations and grief-counseling centers. They helped identify the remains and notify the survivors of the zombie turkey attacks. FEMA provided reunification services for family members lost and scattered in the attack on the 150,000-member community. They also brought all the anti-zombie efforts into unity with a central clearinghouse for information.

Sam and Lisa both contributed to and benefited from the information center.

After working on their stories and updating the website together all that night and into the morning, Sam said, "I need to crash, Lisa. Let's get a couple hotel rooms and take a nap."

"OK, but why do we need the expense of two rooms?"

Embarrassed, Sam said, "Well, we aren't married."

"Doesn't matter to me. I just want to be with you."

"I just wouldn't feel right. I couldn't face my minister, let alone God."

"OK. Let's go to the justice of peace and get married."

"That easy?"

"That easy." They went to the courthouse in downtown Joliet. With the zombie turkey disaster, it was deserted. Within an hour, the justice of peace married them. The janitor and receptionist witnessed the ceremony, signing the wedding certificate.

They drove to the closest motel, where Sam promptly fell asleep.

"You're so romantic, Sam," Lisa said fondly to his snoring form. She was too wound up to sleep. She worried a lot about the *Midley Beacon* and didn't need much sleep anyway. She'd rather work. She filled out the expense report for their dinner and the meal with Liz Latrell. Then she called the webmaster of the *Midley Beacon* and instructed him about her ideas for presenting and formatting the latest videos and stories. She called the printer and made sure he had the evening edition out with the Joliet attacks. They were printing two editions daily, and selling out. She called her email clerk and checked to see if any significant emails had come in. She'd had her email filters set up by sender and filed them into Spam, News Networks, TV, and Important People folders. The email volume was so great she'd abandoned trying to read them herself.

"Hi, Jenny. Any important email come in since I last checked?"

"You got an email from General Bagley. He invited you to the press conference in Joliet City Hall."

"Thanks. When is it?"

"Um, four o'clock."

"Crap! That's fifteen minutes from now! Woah, I'd better go! See ya. Bye."

"Bye."

Good thing she had checked with her staff! The email clerk just paid for her salary. She quickly drove to the Joliet City Hall, where she and Sam had just married a few hours before.

At the press conference, in the city council chamber, General Bagley motioned he would begin.

"At approximately seven p.m. last night, over a hundred thousand zombie turkeys attacked Joliet. They caused widespread death and destruction. The current number of victims is twelve hundred and seventy three, with another eight hundred missing. The Federal Emergency Management Agency is assisting with recovery, notification of the next of kin, and finding lost people." General Bagley spoke somberly to the assembled press.

"The first question to be answered is, how did the turkeys escape our military cordon? The turkeys boarded a string of barges in Hennepin and got off south of Joliet. From there, they went to Farm Fresh Turkey Farm, the largest turkey farm in Illinois, killed the workers there, and infected the seventy thousand turkeys.

"Simultaneously with this barge movement, a parallel attack of a flock of about two thousand zombie turkeys tried to escape the cordon by Spring Bay. They were eliminated by our troops. However, this simultaneous attack probably caused us to not detect the barge moving upstream.

"In response, we are suspending all barge traffic for the duration of this crisis. This zombie outbreak will not happen again," the general asserted firmly.

"The next questions to be answered are, where are the turkeys now, and where will they attack next? Before I address this, let me reintroduce Dr. Edwin Galloway of the Poultry Research Institute in Northwestern University. Dr. Galloway."

"General Bagley invited me here today to share some of our latest findings on this turkey disease, which leads to the condition popularly called 'zombie turkeys.'

"We've managed to induce zombiism in several varieties of turkey. We have also cured the disease in these turkeys, using salt water in various quantities and using various techniques: injection, mist, and bath.

"We have a small flock of zombie turkeys at the Poultry Institute and have tested exactly how much damage they can sustain and still revive. As we already know, chopping a turkey in half, or in smaller pieces, will defeat the regeneration process, as will burning them. However, merely burning their skin is *not* sufficient. Skin and feathers will grow back within hours, and both will be much tougher than normal—enough to stop buckshot smaller than 00. The turkey must be burnt until all the bacteria in it have been sterilized.

"Likewise, chopping off their heads, legs, wings, et cetera, will only cause them to regenerate much stronger than before. Most turkey farms cut off spurs and beaks to prevent damage to the turkeys. When the Farm Fresh turkeys were infected, the beaks and spurs grew back in the hour's journey to Joliet. Even freshly killed turkeys in stores, that have not been frozen, when infected with the bacterium will revive within an hour, growing an entire set of organs. The armed forces are already going through the dead turkeys and chopping each carcass to ensure complete death and prevent resurrection.

"But the most important fact we have discovered is that after feeding, zombie turkeys go into a catatonic state for twenty-four to forty-eight hours. They burrow down in leaf mold or under bushes and twigs while they sleep off their meal. Their body temperature drops, and they are not detectable by infrared detectors. This explains the military's difficulty in tracking them after these attacks. I now turn this conference back over to General Bagley."

"Let me first express my gratitude towards Dr. Galloway and his team at the Poultry Institute. These findings have given us the advantage over our turkey foes. They led directly to the victory at the battle of Spring Bay, and they have given us help in finding the turkeys after the Joliet disaster.

"We are currently tracking the turkeys to their catatonic nests using dogs. We expect to neutralize a majority of these zombie turkeys over the next forty-eight hours. Ladies and gentlemen of the press, the floor is now open to questions."

"Dr. Galloway, what are you doing to prevent future infections of turkeys, wild and domestic? I understand several organic, free-range turkey farms have become infected with zombiism, and all present were lost," asked Jill Holcomb of ABC News.

"At present, the only means of prevention is to daily mist your turkeys with a five percent saline solution. We have not found an effective antibiotic yet. We have informed the Turkey Growers Association of Illinois of this approach," Dr. Galloway said,

"General Bagley, at the last press conference, you said the zombie turkeys wouldn't escape the cordon and had no strategy. Yet they did, and you said the two groups of turkeys moved in tandem, causing you to miss the larger group. Wasn't that a strategy?" asked Ed Fitzgerald of the *Wall Street Journal.*

"No. We discussed the possibility of increased intelligence in the zombie turkeys with Dr. Galloway. He has tested them, and they are not smarter than normal turkeys. However, they do travel in cohesive flocks, larger than natural turkey flocks. We believe that when the turkeys got on the barges, there wasn't enough room for them all, and the flock split. The two flocks still followed the general direction upriver toward the east. What looked like a strategy was just unfortunate happenstance."

"General Bagley, who is fighting on behalf of the zombie turkeys' right to life?" asked an attractive young lady in a trench coat.

Perplexed, General Bagley said, "Excuse me? I don't understand your question, ma'am."

"Turkeys, even zombie turkeys, have as much right to life as human beings do. Even if they're killing people, they have a right to humane deaths. Burning them to death and chopping them to death doesn't qualify as humane deaths!" The woman spoke passionately.

"What news agency are you representing, young lady?" he asked sternly.

"I am the president of the Joliet chapter of People for the Ethical Treatment of Animals! And you, sir, are a turkey murderer!"

"Sergeant, please escort this woman from the press conference," the general commanded. "She's being disruptive."

"You won't silence us that easily!" From a paper bag next to her chair, she took out two water balloons, which she threw at General Bagley and Dr. Galloway. The general and doctor managed to dodge, but the balloons made huge red splotches on the wall. Then, reaching into her trench coat pocket, she pulled out a cylindrical object and hurled it at the general, hitting him in the face with a splat. General Bagley had just been hit by Betty Tuffield's authentic zombie turkey sausage. (May include up to 50 percent filler, not suitable for human consumption.)

"Turkey blood! You have turkey blood on you!" she screamed as the military police dragged her away. The whole room erupted in shouting and yelling. Two PETA supporters near the door handcuffed themselves to the door and then to the PETA president. They all began shouting "Murderers! Murderers! Turkey murderers!" over and over. The PETA supporters shed their trench coats, and they were nude, except for the turkey plumage painted on their bodies.

Uproar filled the conference room. The military police contacted the janitor, who had some bolt cutters.

Humorously, Lisa recognized the janitor as the one who witnessed their wedding. The police cut away the protestors' handcuffs.

A man eating a turkey sandwich cheered on the policemen. "You get'em, guys! Turkeys are good eats!"

"You fat pig! You're too low to be a pig—you're worse than a cannibal! Turkey killer!"

"Better them than me!" the man shouted back.

The officers dragged the three protesters off to jail, wrapped in their coats.

Lisa finished her video recording with that exchange. *This video will draw some eyeballs to our YouTube channel*, she thought. She sent an email to the webmaster to be sure to blur the "naughty bits" from the video. She laughed to herself. Perhaps if they weren't blurred, they'd get even more traffic! But then the networks wouldn't purchase rights to use them. Maybe she could have an exclusive content page just for *Midley Beacon* subscribers? Humming happily to herself, she planned her next business campaign.

Chapter 8

Plattville

Lisa was right. By the time Sam awoke, over a million people had seen the news conference and PETA video. She had a dozen requests to use it worldwide. She sold limited rights to it, as long as the using organization gave the *Midley Beacon* credit. Page hits had become almost as good as cash in the bank.

She now gave away the *Midley Beacon* paper edition for free. The advertising in each issue paid for the printing expenses and still supplied a profit. Each paper had a link to the website and YouTube channel. She printed over a hundred thousand copies a day, sent throughout Illinois and the world. Their primary revenue came from advertisements on YouTube. At the current rate, she'd—she and Sam, that was—make more than a million dollars this year.

"Good evening, Sam. This is Mrs. Melvin. How I love saying that! What is the great reporter's plan?"

"I want supper first. I'm starving."

"Back to the French restaurant?"

"No, that'll always be special. Let's reserve that for special occasions. Let's not overdo it. Let's just eat at the motel restaurant."

Over a steak dinner, Lisa said, "I was serious about where to go next. We can follow up with a report on the Farm Fresh Turkey Farm, or the organic turkey growers association, or be embedded with the military K-9 corps as they track down the hibernating turkeys. Or something else. I trust your instincts."

"Hmm. I definitely want to be embedded with the K-9 corps. I want to find out how many turkeys they find and kill, and hear any scuttlebutt the soldiers have to say. I hate to say this, but we should probably split up. You should follow up on the other two stories."

"What a honeymoon! How romantic you are! We consummate our marriage by splitting up!"

"Take off your romantic wife hat and put on your editor hat. What would the editor of the *Midley Beacon* do?"

"Make love to you and then split up."

"Sounds like a nice compromise!"

They headed back to their motel room. Later, Sam put the expense on their joint trip report.

* * *

That evening, embedded with the K-9 corps, Sam talked with Lieutenant Lou Wallensky, a National Guard volunteer from Chicago who had been pulled into full-time duty for the duration of the zombie turkey crisis. He and Sam both graduated the same year from high school, which helped Sam to build rapport with him. His specialty was working with dogs in the K-9 corps.

"How many turkeys did you find before I joined you?" Sam asked.

"About a thousand."

"Have any troubles, either in finding or killing these turkeys?"

"Not really. The dogs find them. Then we use fixed bayonets to skewer them and then split them with our belt knives. "

"Where are we, exactly? I know we're in the Glen County Forest Preserve, but where?"

"We're at the east end, near Route 83. After we finish here, we go on to Pulaski Woods. We don't want these zombie turkeys to reach Chicago."

"Did you find any more zombie turkeys around Joliet?"

"Yes, the other units report upward of ten thousand hibernating turkeys found and destroyed."

"Hmm. That's eleven thousand, maybe twelve thousand with those you've found since I've joined you. That's still ninety thousand turkeys unaccounted for."

"We're assuming those have not hibernated but have migrated."

"To where?"

"We're still searching."

* * *

Lisa left the Farm Fresh Turkey Farm that evening. There had not been much to find out. She'd captured some video of the ravaged pens and farm. Unlike the organic turkey farms, it was much more a factory-style facility. The turkeys had been jammed together in cages, which they had torn to pieces when they went zombie. She decided to juxtapose this turkey farm report with the *Beacon*'s PETA video.

On the way to the Farm Fresh Turkey Farm, she'd talked with Fletcher Axel and his wife. They'd warmed up to her and Sam, and they now trusted them enough to give them the phone numbers and addresses to all the organic turkey farmers in the area.

To protect the organic survivalist farmers' secrecy, she'd had to promise not to give out names and locations of those not conquered by the zombie turkeys. The big find had been additional contact names of other organic turkey farmers who were not in their network but whom they knew. She'd visit each of them.

She and Sam joined up late that night. They didn't get much sleep before they got up early in the morning to check out the various turkey farms, but they didn't mind. Some things were more important than sleep.

The first farm they visited was west of Oglesby. The mail box said *The Smiths'*. Ominously, the front door hung open. Turkey feathers covered the ground like snow. Spots of blood dotted the ground here and there, but they found no bodies, human or turkey. They did find a couple of bullet holes and some empty shotgun shells.

"Pretty grim," Sam commented. "Do you think anyone survived?"

"Maybe. Let's see if we can figure how many turkeys they had." The turkey sheds were like big chicken coops. The arrangement differed from Fletcher Axel's big barn, but the quantity of turkey cages seemed about the same, about five hundred.

There was no car in the garage. The family seemed to have fled.

"I'll call General Bagley. Let's go to the next place."

From Oglesby they motored up I-39 to Troy Grove. West of there they found Junger Meyer's larger, intact farm. The Meyers greeted them. Sam and Lisa passed on the warning about the zombie turkeys and the usefulness of salt water, harrows, flamethrowers, axes, and chainsaws.

Junger said, "Thanks a million! What can I do to repay you?"

"Here's our business card," Lisa said. "Subscribe for free to the *Midley Beacon* and our website. You'll find lots of useful information and products there."

They had a new viewer of their YouTube and online newspaper. Looking intently at his tablet as he surfed their site, Junger said, "Hey, these Tom's Turkey Traps look pretty good."

"They are," Sam said. "I personally saw and documented the results. Look up 'Tom Tuffield Traps Take Down Turkeys' on our site for the complete report, with video."

Sam and Lisa were quite fond of that story and their ability to sell traps from the *Midley* website. After a delicate conversion with Mrs. Tuffield, Sam had persuaded her to pay 10 percent of the traps' profits to the paper. She agreed the *Midley Beacon*'s advertising was worth the money and had made a testimonial on the paper's behalf. That, plus their voluminous web traffic, caused hundreds of companies to request and then to beg to advertise on their site. Lisa believed in "skimming the cream off the top," so she charged top dollar for the top-story pages. Lisa also instituted profit sharing for the employees. Basically, she divided the weekly profits from the website equally among everyone working at the paper. This served as a massive inducement for all the reporters to advertise their paper and its products.

While discussing the profits from traps, they drove from the Meyers at Troy Grove, to the Wilburs at Wedron, to the Bakers at Lisbon, to the McGillicuddys north of Plattville. The McGillicuddys were the next victims. Mrs. Wilma McGillicuddy and her children had survived in the family bomb shelter, but her husband, John, had died fighting off the turkeys. He'd used a Thompson submachine gun and his shotgun, but the turkeys had overwhelmed him. He'd bled to death after crawling to their shelter. The thousand turkeys on the farm flew the coop, except for some shredded turkeys. Sam and Lisa gave them solace and connections to Mrs. Yoder and Mrs. Tuffield. Those two had formed the Zombie Turkey Widows Help Association (ZoTWHA). The ZoTWHA dedicated itself to helping zombie widows recover from the shocking death of their spouses and get reestablished financially. Sam and Lisa also gave Mrs. McGillicuddy contact names and numbers at FEMA, who would also help them.

Sam and Lisa traveled from Plattville to Oswego, and they visited the Hillers' farm, run by brothers Andy and Arthur Hiller. No zombie turkeys there. The brothers were relieved to find out a saline solution prevented the infection. They already had a flamethrower they used for clearing brush.

On the east side of Joliet, west of Manhattan, they found another ruined, abandoned farm. About a thousand turkeys had turned zombie. The Samson family had fled. South of there, west of Maneno, another lost farm. Seven hundred turkeys belonging to the Williams had escaped. Fortunately, so had the Williams—most of them. Hank Williams (named after the singer) had three teenage children but lost his wife in the attack. She had been in the barn feeding the turkeys when they turned zombie.

Sam and Lisa also gave him the ZoTWHA contact information. Sam thought widowers needed help too.

They continued until dark, hitting ten of the fourteen farms on their list. Five had lost their turkeys, four thousand in total. Only the McGillicuddys were still on their farm. Sam plotted the farms on a map. The farms around Joliet had all been lost. They had called General Bagley about the lost ones, and they had warned the ones that had not been lost. They had also learned of ten more small organic turkey farms from the survivors.

Sam wrote up a news report about the farms and attacks, carefully hiding the locations and names of the families. The video they had taken accompanied the report.

Meanwhile, Joliet had received a lot of help in searching for and fighting turkeys. Several Chicago street gangs came down, offering to "'busta cap' in a bird." They were well armed with handguns, machine pistols, and submachine guns, as well as switchblades. Neither the National Guard nor the Joliet police department wanted to deal with the tattooed, gang sign-waving, gang clothing-wearing groups. However, the local militia groups just treated them like another militia group and directed them accordingly. The various militia groups gathered daily to share what they had learned, what turkeys they had killed, whether they were hibernating or alive, and where they had gone. They used a map of Illinois at their headquarters, the local NRA (National Rifle Association) office. The Chicago gangs, the People and the Folk, were directed to unexplored areas around Joliet, and met with the rest of the militia every evening. They provided additional manpower and intelligence. As they killed turkeys, they took to wearing the wattles as part of their gang colors. The more proficient among them were completely covered in wattles.

Aside from Chicago street gangs, gun clubs across the state gathered in Joliet to search for zombie turkeys and kill them. They brought plenty of unusual weaponry: large shotguns, elephant guns, explosive shells, black powder rifles, and Civil War–replica cannons. There were even rounds of shrapnel and buckshot designed to be shot from these cannons.

The militia also exchanged hunting and shooting tips and gun advice. They set up informal barter and sale of guns in the NRA headquarters, specifically on the bulletin board. There you'd see things like *Need 7.62 x 51 mm ammo; anyone got any?*, *Will trade 1911 .45 ammo for new firing pin for M82 machine gun*, and *Wanted badly: .30-06 carbine. Will trade hunting dog or wife for it.*

Other than these developments, not much had been happening in Joliet, aside from the rebuilding work. The K-9 corps had found a few thousand more hibernating turkeys, and the soldiers destroyed them. The lost turkey farms had more than made up for the hibernating zombie turkey losses. The other ninety thousand turkeys had simply vanished—again.

* * *

"This isn't much of a honeymoon for you, Lisa," Sam said, as they hit the sack after another enervating day.

"It's an ideal honeymoon—love and work."
"Wow. What did I do to deserve to get you?"
"You are yourself. That's enough for me."
And so to bed.

* * *

While Sam and Lisa were engaged in connubial bliss, Hank Williams looked up ZoTWHA on the internet. He no longer felt stunned about the loss of his wife; it was like an impacted toothache in his heart. He had contacted his local mortuary, which had gathered her remains. He had their glossy brochure with its list of funeral options before him, all more than he could afford, especially now that he'd lost all his turkeys. His teen daughters were crying, and his son was sullen and withdrawn. He turned to the internet to escape. He didn't really think ZoTWHA could help.

He started reading the ZoTWHA blog, written by Helen Yoder. She captured his emptiness and grief. Maybe they *could* help him.

He signed up for their blog subscription. He also checked out Tom's Turkey Traps. They could've really helped him, had he known. He had heard about the zombie plague, but it didn't seem real, and it was way off downstate from him. He read in the ad that the proceeds helped the ZoTWHA. That decided him. He immediately ordered the wood chipper and the apocalypse trap. He'd be getting his shipment of turkeys soon. He'd order them as soon as he got a check from the insurance company. No sense in repeating his mistake.

Hmmm. Betty Tuffield was the CEO of Tom's Turkey Traps Inc. There was a link to her story on the *Midley Beacon*. Woah! Tom had had all these traps, and he still died. Oddly, that made Hank feel better. He'd felt guilty since his wife's death—that he should have been able to prevent it. Now he knew if your name was written on a zombie turkey, you couldn't avoid death.

* * *

That same day in downtown Chicago, over a hundred members of the local NRA chapter marched in front of the Chicago city hall. Starting at noon on the three week days before Thanksgiving, they carried signs: *Guns Kill Zombies!,*

The 2nd Amendment Gives the Right to Be Zombie Free, and *Give Me Guns or Give Me Death by Zombies.* The protestors also carried petitions for the city council to relax the gun ordinances for Chicago and for Cook County for the duration of the zombie turkey crisis. Mayor Rahm Emanuel met with them.

"I understand your concerns," he said, "but I also have concerns—gun deaths in Chicago are among the nation's highest. We must protect our citizens, especially our youth."

"Don't you think the gun deaths are caused by your unconstitutional restrictions on guns?" asked the local NRA chapter president, Wallace William, also known as "Wally."

"Our laws have been upheld by the courts!" protested the mayor.

"Regardless, we're not asking for anything that's not guaranteed by the Constitution: the right to bear and carry arms in self-defense."

The mayor responded, "I've talked with you. Now go." That caused a huge shout of protest. The NRA members continued their protest and to collect signatures that day and the next.

On Wednesday, before Thanksgiving, they placed their petitions, with over two hundred thousand signatures from Chicago and Cook County citizens, before the mayor in city hall. All the major media—newspapers, radio, television, and internet bloggers who had been following the protest— covered the event.

Somewhat stunned by the volume of the petitions, and realizing they represented a significant voting bloc, the mayor promised, "We will verify if these signatures are genuine, and if so, we will consider relaxing the gun laws for the duration of the zombie turkey crisis." This statement elicited a big cheer.

But the NRA president, Wally, said, "We need protection *now.* The citizens of Chicago need to defend themselves against zombies *now.* We want action *now*! How many deaths will it take, Mr. Mayor, before you let Chicago citizens exercise their constitutional right to self-defense?"

"Of course they can do that *now.* Chicago citizens can have weapons in their homes for self-defense."

"We need open carry! We don't want any restrictions on the size of magazines," Wally shouted. Dozens of other NRA members echoed him loudly.

"That will be brought up to the city council, I promise," the mayor said placatingly. The NRA members began chanting, "Hell no, turkeys must go!"

This televised and internet-streamed confrontation, and the three-day protest, excited many gun owners and would-be gun owners. Those who had no weapons went out and bought shotguns that day. Those who already had weapons bought more and started carrying them in their vehicles. Others, realizing that flamethrowers and chainsaws weren't mentioned in the conference or in the law, ordered those. Express shipping services delivered thousands of flamethrowers and chainsaws to Chicago on Thanksgiving Day.

* * *

The day before Thanksgiving, Hank Williams called ZoTWHA. He didn't like all the touchy-feely crap that he associated with help lines and help groups, but he was desperate. His children were grieving deeply over their mother and didn't even want to have a Thanksgiving dinner. He felt they *needed* to celebrate Thanksgiving, no matter what.

"Hello, this is the Zombie Turkey Widows Help Association," answered a deep contralto voice.

"Hello, this is Hank Williams. I wonder if you can help me. I lost my wife in a zombie turkey attack a couple of days ago, and my children don't want to celebrate Thanksgiving. Sam and Lisa Melvin suggested I contact your organization."

"Oh! I know Sam Melvin. He comforted me when my husband, Amos, died. I'm Helen Yoder."

"I really liked your blog posts. You captured my feelings exactly."

"Thank you. Regarding your Thanksgiving problem with your children, your whole family can come to a Thanksgiving dinner ZoTWHA is having at Betty Tuffield's farm in Henry. We chose that place because it is centrally located."

"Thanks for the invitation, but I can't see how that will help. My kids aren't thankful for anything after their mother's death. That's why they don't want to celebrate Thanksgiving."

"That's exactly the point. They need to be thankful for their mother. All of us in ZoTWHA will remember our lost spouses at this Thanksgiving and celebrate their memories."

"That's a good idea! I'll get them there! What time should we come over? Should we bring anything?"

"There's no need to bring anything. We've already got more food than we can eat. You can arrive as early as twelve p.m., if you want to help with the preparation. We'll be both roasting and frying turkeys."

"I've done both before. I'll be glad to help. It'll do my kids good to help out too."

"I'm looking forward to seeing you there, Hank, with your kids!"

"Me too! I haven't felt this good since Laurie's death."

After he hung up, Hank immediately explained the plan to his children. They were dubious but willing to give it a try. They liked the idea of being thankful for their mother. Maybe this Thanksgiving wouldn't be as bad as he feared.

Chapter 9

Chicago

The list of conquered turkey farms the Melvins had given General Bagley led him to search every farm in the area overnight. He found the ten turkey farms the Melvins had learned of, all of them zombified. Another mega turkey farm in Tinley Hills had been overthrown. A truck delivering live turkeys for Thanksgiving to the farm for slaughter had gone zombie, and then the whole farm. A major battlefront erupted in Tinley Hills, with sixty thousand rampaging zombie turkeys. The National Guard dispatched five thousand troops there and called in the marines to help.

The zombie turkey plague metastasized. Multiple flocks of thousands of turkeys rampaged across the Illinois countryside. Ninety thousand turkeys had disappeared from Joliet. The rush for guns, weapons, knives, axes, flamethrowers, and chainsaws gushed into a tidal wave in Illinois and the neighboring states. Hardware stores, farm stores, and gun shops sold out of guns and ammo, axes, and chainsaws. The YouTube videos showing how to make napalm secured millions of hits.

Even citizens of the gun-controlled zones of Chicago and Cook County armed themselves to the teeth. An unprecedented security force surrounded Soldier Field for the big Thanksgiving Day game between the Chicago Bears and the Green Bay Packers. The city, state, and federal governments, along with the NFL, debated about cancelling the game due to the zombie turkeys, but the Chicago police force, in coordination with the National Guard and the US

Army and Marines, assured the city officials they could keep Chicago safe. The NFL also did not want to cancel one of its biggest-rated games on the off chance of zombie turkeys.

The crowd arrived at Soldier Field with hidden knives, guns, chainsaws, and flamethrowers. The Soldier Field security crew let them in with a wink and a nod. They did confiscate hidden food and drink though. The food vendors had to make a living.

* * *

He felt great. He had a vague memory of being shredded by fléchette. He would have to lead his flock away from those predators. The other memories of dying had already faded. He had found many caves in which they could hide, one after another—some filled with captive turkeys. They freed them and killed a few predators.

Cave after cave after cave of turkeys, all in a row. The predators closed them into the caves but didn't attack. This puzzled him. Then the caves started to shift, like the moving island, only moving caves. There were many things he didn't know, but one thing he could do. He bred with the hens in his cave.

After the caves stopped shifting, quiet settled for a long time. They were hungry and thirsty in these caves. Then the caves opened. Predators.

The turkeys attacked and killed them. "Gobble! Gobble!"

That sated their hunger.

He could smell water not far away and led his flock there.

It was dark. The ground was hard rock with just a few patches of grass. The rock went right down to the river. They found ledges on which to drink during this quiet time at night, with few predators. But steady noise buzzed in the background as predators gathered around the moving caves.

The flock was huge. They could kill many predators. He still felt the need to hide, because he felt surrounded. He was also sleepy from the heavy meal of meat.

He led his flock down the river. There were many places to conceal themselves, overhangs and cliffs, but not enough for the whole flock. Occasionally, they'd find a predator and eat him. So they had food and water. He felt the urge to hide before daylight, before too many predators became active.

They reached a huge pool of water, too big to see or fly across. There was much greenery and many tunnels. Sometimes predators lurked in the tunnels, but they were sleeping and were easy meat. The turkeys slept in the bushes and tunnels by the water.

The many predators woke them up. The tom and his flock ate some, but they were surrounded. He led his flock away, following the greenery by the big pool of water. He saw a small meadow with just a few predators. Good eats! He led his flock there.

* * *

The crowds filled Soldier Field. Over a hundred buses came from Wisconsin, bearing Packers fans. Just after kickoff at 1:00 p.m., the sky grew dark. An enormous flock of turkeys flew into the stadium and covered the field. An endless cacophony of "Gobble! Gobble!" rose from the stadium.

* * *

"This is the Emergency Alert System. This is *not* a test. Repeat, this is *not* a test. This is an actual civil emergency. The federal government has declared a state of emergency over the entire state of Illinois due to the zombie turkey crisis.

"Zombie turkeys have attacked the Soldier Field Stadium and downtown Chicago. National Guard officials believe the turkeys escaped from Joliet on a freight train full of domestic turkeys for Thanksgiving and debarked at the Chicago LaSalle station. Dozens of downtown Chicago pedestrians and homeless people have been eaten. The Illinois National Guard, in conjunction with the marines, army, and air force, is conducting military operations against the turkeys.

"Approximately one hundred fifty thousand domestic turkeys have gone zombie, and approximately one hundred thousand wild turkeys. The National Turkey Institute has bred zombie turkeys and discovered their growth cycle is vastly accelerated. The eggs hatch faster, the poults grow faster, and the new zombie turkeys are dangerous within three weeks. There are an estimated one hundred thousand new zombie turkeys added to the flocks ravaging Illinois since the plague began at the beginning of November.

"Furthermore, not only are the zombie turkeys resistant to damage, and not only do they regenerate quickly, but once regenerated, they are two to three times stronger than normal turkeys.

"Citizens are advised to stay within their homes. Those with bunkers or air-raid shelters should stay in them until further notice. Those on the road to Illinois are advised to stop and return home. The federal government has stopped all road, sea, and air traffic to Illinois. The US Army, Marines, and Air Force are currently conducting operations against the zombie turkeys and expect to eliminate them within a week.

"Civilians should use salt water spray on any attacking turkeys, or tranquilizer guns loaded with salt water. Salt water is highly effective in stopping the zombie plague.

"That is all."

* * *

On Thanksgiving, the eTurkey delivery truck arrived at the Indian Turkey Farm in Brimel, Indiana, with the delivery of 110 live turkeys: fifteen Eastern wild turkeys, fifteen Osceola wild turkeys, thirty-five Standard Bronze, thirty Blue Slate, and fifteen Bourbon Red. Aaron Root, the receiving quality manager, inspected each one carefully. They were all healthy poults; they had never gotten a bad turkey from eTurkey. However, one turkey seemed to have an eye infection; its eyes were red. He treated it with antiseptic.

Aaron sighed with satisfaction. It was great eTurkey delivered on Thanksgiving. After selling so many turkeys for Thanksgiving, they had to build their supply up for Christmas and New Year's. Modern technology had really made breeding and raising turkeys much easier. He could hardly wait to see what happened next. Automated truck deliveries by self-driving trucks? He put the new turkeys in their pens, with the other turkeys.

* * *

Sam and Lisa had planned to take Thanksgiving off for a honeymoon in Joliet. Lisa said that since they were on a work-related trip, they could expense the holiday to the paper. In their motel room in Joliet, they were watching the Thanksgiving Day football game when a cloud of zombie turkeys descended upon Soldier Field. The emergency alert caused them to scan the internet for breaking stories about zombie turkeys.

Sam went from website to website, tracking the zombie turkey attacks on his laptop. "Tinley Park...Soldier Field...Chicago Loop. A new flock has appeared near Joliet. Princeville has also been attacked again. Bartonville...Peoria," he read off to Lisa.

"I never thought I'd say this, Sam, but I think the story has gotten too big for the *Midley Beacon*. I've added a zombie turkey Twitter feed to our site, but this is way too big for us to be everywhere, even with the six new reporters I've hired. I've sent one to Bartonville and Peoria, one to Princeville, two to Joliet, one to Tinley Park, and one to Chicago. Chicago alone should have six reporters."

"Well, let's go to Chicago then. Three are better than one."

"I'm with you on that. Lemme give Charlie a call. He's our guy in Chicago."

She called Charlie Gomez. "Hi, Charlie, where are you?" Lisa frowned.

"Speak up! I can barely hear you... Oh, keep your head down then... We'll cover the Loop activity then... OK, good reporting. Stay alive! Report daily or more often! Bye."

"What's up with Charlie?"

"He's in the middle of the zombie turkey firefight in Soldier Field. It's quite a melee there. Let's go to the Loop."

Normally, during rush hour, the trip to the Loop could take up to two hours from Joliet. On Thanksgiving, with traffic down because of the holiday and the civil emergency, and Sam's heavy foot on the pedal, it took less than one. They passed through several military checkpoints, where they had to show their press badges. On their way to Chicago, they heard another emergency broadcast.

"The is the Emergency Alert System. This is *not* a test. Repeat, this is *not* a test. This is an actual civil emergency. The federal government has declared a state of emergency over the entire United States due to the zombie turkey crisis. In addition to the estimated three hundred and fifty thousand zombie turkeys in Illinois, another hundred and fifty thousand live turkeys have been shipped through the eTurkey service around the country. If you have received any turkeys from eTurkey, do not let them loose. Approximately one hundred percent of these eTurkeys have turned zombie. Repeat, do not accept any live turkeys from eTurkey."

* * *

President Barack Obama, his wife, Michelle, and their children, Malia and Sasha, and some close friends, among them Chicago Mayor Rahm Emanuel, sat down to dinner at the president's Chicago home in the Kenwood suburb. The White House chef, Philippe Lavoisier, had prepared fresh roasted wild turkey stuffed with wild rice for the party of twelve and the twelve Secret Service agents protecting them. The Secret Service crew had been beefed up in light of the zombie turkey plague. They had advised the President against going to Chicago, but he wanted to show fearlessness in the face of the turkeys and that the federal government had the crisis well under control. They also had Marine Helicopter Squadron One (HMX-1), known as "Marine One," in case of a need for evacuation.

The whole party was watching the battle of Soldier Field on the big-screen TV, when the turkey was brought into the dining room. In addition to the roast turkey, stuffed with sage-flavored wild rice and glazed with pomegranate sauce, the meal included cranberries, twice-baked garlic mashed potatoes in the potato skins, and brown sugar–coated yams, asparagus, green beans, and corn on the cob.

"That smells delicious!" the president said.

"You can say that again!" said Rahm Emanuel.

"It is delicious!" the First Lady said after tasting it. "Where did you get the turkey, Philippe?"

"It's a high-tech innovation. It was freshly delivered alive, yesterday. There's an online company that delivers live turkeys. It's an Eastern wild turkey."

"What's the name of the company?" the president asked.

"eTurkey."

* * *

In Soldier Field, the din of the fans, the yelling of the players, and the ceaseless "Gobble! Gobble!" of the zombie turkeys assaulted Charlie Gomez's ears. He began his reporting in the stands, narrating the action as he recorded and streamed it via video camera. The sixty-two thousand fans in the stadium hindered the National Guard, army, and marines in fighting the turkeys. In the stands, thousands of fans fought the turkeys with knives and axes they had smuggled into the stadium. One fan would wound a turkey, and then dozens of others would jump on the wounded turkey, slicing it into many pieces. The knowledge that zombie turkeys had to be at least split in two to stop the regenerating process was known nationally and worldwide by now.

Fans clambered over seats and up and down aisles to reach turkeys as they perched there. For once, people outnumbered turkeys. Fans quickly slaughtered all of the flock that landed in the stands.

Charlie made sure he recorded both Bear and Packer fans. He had to maintain his journalistic impartiality at this important historic event.

* * *

Meanwhile, in the Pentagon, the Joint Chiefs of Staff somberly discussed their various options in responding to the mass outbreak of zombie turkeys, especially the attack around and within Soldier Field. In the secret, high-tech war room beneath the building, a huge video screen showed a map of the US marked with the latest turkey sightings and the nation's armed forces arrayed. The US forces were tracked by GPS signals in each vehicle. The turkey sightings were updated real time. As they watched, several new red turkey icons appeared in Illinois, each one signaling an outbreak. The size of the turkey icon indicated the number of turkeys, from a thousand to a hundred thousand. An adjacent screen showed Soldier Field and the battle there.

The top air force general advocated, "Let's do a napalm strike on the field. That'll wipe them out. We can use our smart bombs, and we can place them within a yard of any point on the field."

The leading general of the army suggested, "Let's have a strafing run with fléchette-armored helicopters. We have prepared a hundred thousand rounds of the new salt water–injecting fléchettes. We can be accurate within a foot."

The marine general said, "We need to rappel a battalion of marines from helicopters to the field. They are accurate with their fléchette rocket launchers within an inch."

The secretary of defense listened to the debate while watching the melee in the stadium. He noticed the success of the fans with their weapons and said, "Men, I think we should give the US citizens a chance to attack the turkeys with their own weapons. I don't want to kill any citizens through collateral damage. However, let's prepare for the marine assault should it be necessary. And besides, I'm a Packer fan. I don't want to harm my team."

Back at Soldier Field, despite the success of the bloodthirsty fans in the stands, the majority of the flock, perhaps sixty thousand, had landed on the field. The fans near the field enthusiastically attacked the zombies with knives and axes and even a few chainsaws. The chainsaws had been smuggled into the stadium inside of violin cases, supposedly to play the national anthem.

The football players, ninety strong between the two teams, united to provide a line of protection between the turkeys and the fans on the field. The fans shared their extra axes and knives with the players, who energetically wielded them against the pressing flock of kicking, pecking turkeys. Their football uniforms, with their hands taped and gloved, with helmets and mouth guards and face shields, made the players almost invulnerable to the turkeys' attacks. Several big linemen hacked through the turkeys with chainsaws, like combines in a wheat field. Other players used multiple ceramic knives, one in each hand. Designed for sushi, these knives effectively bifurcated a turkey with a single stroke.

The biggest danger for the football players was tripping over the growing mounds of split turkeys and falling beneath the zombies' razor-sharp spurs, or being knocked down by the ravening hordes of living zombie turkeys mindlessly charging their predators. A secondary danger was slashing a fellow football player with a knife or chainsaw. After some players lost padding through near misses with chainsaws, the players spread themselves about ten feet apart around most of the flock. Each wielded two knives, or axes, or chainsaws. Fans backed up the players as they advanced into the turkey flock. The players whirled and swung, chopped and sliced, like gigantic food processors.

By the time the turkeys in front realized the danger, the players sliced each in two or more pieces. The pressure of the flock of turkeys behind them kept pushing new turkeys into the fray. The crazed and frenzied fans behind the players hacked any turkeys that ran or flew past the line of protection. The fans happily supported their teams in turkey butchery. The Packers fans backed up their team, and the Bears fans backed up their team.

Although the players were top-notch athletes, continuously chopping turkeys for ten, fifteen, and twenty minutes left them weary. One gigantic lineman yelled "Man, I could use a timeout!" before a clot of twenty or thirty turkeys attacked him. Dozens of fans, less athletic but more numerous, quickly sliced the turkeys off the player, peeling them off with their knives as if skinning an apple.

More fans worked their way down to the field, filling in the space as the turkey flock slowly contracted. The fans cheered the players on from the stands and the field, encouraging them to keep up the butchery despite their leaden arms. Although no football game took place, everyone remained in the stadium, either participating in the zombie turkey battle or caught up in the excitement of watching the players' gladiatorial contest with the paranormal birds.

Thirty minutes of continuous avian death reduced the flock to half its original size, but the exhausted players could barely hold up their knives or chainsaws to defend themselves. Meanwhile, the military helicopters circling the field shot fléchettes into any turkeys flying out of the stadium.

The copter pilots noticed the flagging players and radioed headquarters for reinforcements. A firefighting plane went over the field and dumped thousands of gallons of salt water on the remaining turkeys. Stunned, startled, and wet, the dezombified turkeys stopped their mindless assault, suddenly vulnerable to the tired players, and more so, to the zealous fans, who shouted, "Kill them! Kill them all! Let Alton Brown sort them out!"

A wave of screaming fans surged past the football players to the dazed and unzombified turkeys. Thousands of fans killed tens of thousands of turkeys. Sadly, collateral damage occurred through friendly fire—some fans cut others with the swirling knives. Those clad only in their team-colored war paint suffered the most cuts and gashes. However, most wore heavy winter coats due to the Chicago weather, which protected them from accidental cuts. Over ten thousand fans on the field quickly wiped out the remaining thirty thousand turkeys in an orgy of turkey gore.

A spirit of joy and camaraderie filled the stadium. The victory over the zombie turkeys felt rather like winning the Super Bowl, or at least winning the Bears versus Packers game. Even Bear and Packer fans embraced and celebrated. Charlie Gomez caught it all on video and uploaded files to YouTube while streaming and narrating the action on Periscope. The excited fans tore down the goal posts to celebrate.

No one knew who started it, but one stentorian fan began singing the Thanksgiving song "Over the River and through the Wood," and soon the whole stadium was singing it, knee deep in turkey blood and guts:

> Over the river and through the wood
> To Grandmother's house we go.
> The horse knows the way to carry the sleigh
> Through white and drifted snow.
>
> Over the river and through the wood,
> Oh, how the wind does blow.
> It stings the toes and bites the nose
> As over the ground we go.
>
> Over the river and through the wood,
> Now Grandma's cap I spy.
> Hurrah for fun; the pudding's done;
> Hurrah for the pumpkin pie.

And once the crowd finished these verses, they started again. Charlie videoed and uploaded this festive celebration. (Of all the videos he uploaded that day, this one went viral.

Tens of millions of people around the world learned the words to "Over the River and Through the Wood." Over the next few months, "Hurrah for the pumpkin pie" would eventually become internet slang for a complete and total slaughter of a foe.)

The crowd stopped singing when a cloud darkened the sun; it was another flock of one hundred thousand turkeys. The flock from Tinley Park had arrived, driven off by the US military there and fleeing west. Although they did not land near Soldier Field, their ominous shadow disturbed the throng. As a result, the crowd finally listened to the public address system's pleas for them to evacuate the stadium, and filed out. Turkey blood and feathers covered many fans. Although they had not seen a football game, they all felt they had gotten their money's worth of violence.

* * *

Rulon Miller was a turkey and duck hunter who lived on the south side of Chicago. He loved the show *Duck Dynasty*. He owned their branded camo gear. He had bought twelve different Duck Commander duck calls, and he had made three special calls for turkeys. One was for toms: *Gobble! Gobble!* One was for hens: *gobble! gobble!* And one was a universal call that attracted them all: *GOBBLE! GOBBLE!* He went turkey or duck hunting every weekend he could. In this manner, he refined his turkey calls until turkeys couldn't resist them. He planned to market them and become rich, just like the Robertsons on *Duck Dynasty*. Then maybe he could marry. Of course, he had to find a girl first.

Rulon heard the Emergency Alert System warnings about the zombie turkeys attacking downtown Chicago. Chicago was now a target-rich environment, and it was open season on turkeys! He could go hunting right here in Chicago! He had read about zombie turkeys on the internet, from the *Midley Beacon*, the definitive source for all things zombie turkey, so he already was fully prepared for killing them.

He packed for his hunting trip carefully. He took all three of his turkey calls and his three shotguns—the Remington pump, the Mossberg Magnum, and the Winchester Pump. He took all his 00 shot magnum shells he used for home defense—five hundred rounds of 12 gauge. *Chicago is my home, and I'm defending it!* he thought. He put on all his camo clothing: shirt, jacket, pants, boots, socks, underwear. He had no flamethrower or chainsaw, but he took his bowie knife and an axe. He put the guns in his gun rack on his pickup truck, and the ammo and axe in the chrome tool chest. Finally, he put his camouflaged *Duck Dynasty* cup, filled with hot black coffee, in the cup holder on the dash, and took off to the north, looking for a flock of zombie turkeys.

* * *

Hank Williams and his three children—Lauren, seventeen; Ryan, fifteen; and Rachel, thirteen—arrived at Tom's Turkeys farm promptly at noon. There were several cars already parked in the drive.

"Here we are!" Hank tried to stir up his children's enthusiasm. He got a "Hmmpf!" from Lauren, and silence from Ryan and Rachel.

A sturdy brown-haired woman greeted them at the front door. "Hello. You must be Hank Williams."

Looking into clear, hazel eyes, he said, "And you must be Betty Tuffield. I've already talked with Helen Yoder, and your voice is different."

Betty laughed. "Yes, Helen has that beautiful voice, so she's a natural for the ZoTWHA phone. She's pretty shy, but she doesn't mind talking on the phone. I'm the designated greeter," she said with a smile.

"I was really impressed with Tom's Turkey Traps. I've already ordered two."

"Yes, Tom put his whole heart into them and protecting this farm. That's what I'm thankful for today."

Her voice and firm mouth didn't waver, but Hank heard a tiny pause between sentences. He felt a surge of empathy for her, knowing exactly how she felt.

"Here, let me introduce you to everyone."

Betty introduced them to Wilma McGuillicuddy and her three teenage sons. They had also arrived early to help. Lauren and Rachel immediately perked up. Even Ryan started horsing around with the teens.

With his children engaged and positive, Hank felt a great weight removed from his shoulders. He happily toured with

Betty around the farm. The turkey barn was now a sausage factory.

"They say you never want to see sausage being made," Hank commented.

"Trust me—that's nothing compared with a zombie turkey attack," Betty said grimly.

"Don't I know it!" Hank agreed.

Betty stopped and looked at him intently. "Of course. You would know." She sounded pleased.

They returned to the farmhouse and began preparations for Thanksgiving. Five families would be there: Helen Yoder, her son, and his family of four; Betty; the Williams; the McGuillicuddys; and last to arrive, the Jenkins. Mary Jenkins, a young widow from Oswego Organic Farm, had four children ranging from two to ten. When Mary, a harried blonde, came in, she said, "Sorry! We're running late."

Betty smiled. "No problem. We're just starting the preparations. What would you like to do?"

"I've made the stuffing. Bill loved it." Her voice caught at the mention of her deceased spouse.

Betty hugged her. "You're in the right place. We're all thankful for our spouses."

Hank met Helen last. She had been with her son and three grandchildren in the recreation room downstairs.

"I finally get to meet Hank Williams."

"And I get to meet the woman with the lovely voice!"

Helen blushed and looked down. "Thank you." She introduced him to her son, daughter-in-law, and grandchildren. He introduced her to his children. Surprisingly, the teens took to the younger children and occupied them with air hockey and Ping-Pong.

Hank got the turkey fryer going. As the oil heated up, he checked the Bears-Packers game on his tablet. A lifelong Bears fan, he never missed the Thanksgiving game.

Dumbfounded, he couldn't believe the video. Clouds of turkeys attacked thousands of fans and players.

"Hey, everyone! Look at this!"

Betty turned on the large-screen TV in the rec room, and in amazement they all watched the *Midley Beacon*'s streaming video of the battle of Soldier Field.

Then a klaxon horn went off in the farmhouse.

"Crap and a half!" Betty exclaimed.

"What's that? A fire?" Hank asked.

"Don't I wish! It's a zombie turkey attack."

* * *

"Mr. President?" the lead Secret Service agent, Agent Smith, asked deferentially.

"Yes, Smith?"

"The eTurkey company is a known vector for zombie turkeys. I recommend evacuation from Chicago now."

"Smith, there's the turkey on the table, and I'm successfully attacking it with my knife and fork now."

"Chef Philippe, are there any live turkeys around here?"

"No, Agent Smith. I plucked and slaughtered fifteen turkeys yesterday. We baked three for the dinner today."

"Where are the other twelve?"

"Ha-ha. You realize they have no heads or guts, right?" Confronting the stone-faced agent, wearing dark glasses, with his suit bulging from muscles and his pistol, Chef Philippe reconsidered his answer. "Oh, you're serious? They're in the walk-in cooler in the main kitchen."

"Agent Robinson, come with me, please."

"Yes, sir."

The two burly agents walked downstairs to the main kitchen. The walk-in cooler, a cool room kept at forty degrees, about six by eight, lined with shelves, adjoined the kitchen and was sealed by a refrigerator door. They opened the sealed door, and twelve zombie turkeys attacked.

"Gobble! Gobble!"

Agent Smith lost his sunglasses, an eye, and got gouged in the face. Agent Robinson fired his gun and knocked down two turkeys. The rest flew past and fluttered upstairs.

Hearing gunshots, the remaining ten agents split. Four went to the corridor to the kitchen, and six hustled the president and his family to Marine One. No debate or negotiation occurred; the presidential family's lives were in danger. The other eight guests fled in terror to their cars and then headed home, their Thanksgiving meal cut short by a turkey counterattack.

In the hallway, four agents fired a fusillade against the oncoming turkeys. Four more dropped, and two were winged.

Still, six turkeys flew past them and into the dining room. Two agents remained to dispatch the six downed turkeys with their military service knives, while two agents went to the dining room. Agent Robinson joined them. He had already split the two turkeys downed in the kitchen.

The three agents picked off the zombie turkeys in the dining room, carefully firing from the doorway. The turkeys pecked at the discarded turkey dinner ravenously. "Gobble! Gobble!" Six, seven shots: the turkeys fell to expert shooting, although still wriggling. A quick bisection with the agents' Navy SEAL knives finished off the six turkeys.

Agent Smith radioed in, his face bandaged and bloody: "House clear. Don Ho, Betty Boop, Jasmine, and Pocahontas are all away."

"Marine One here. We're going down in the Loop and getting the president under cover. We're encountering heavy, and I mean *heavy*, turkey flocks. We cannot stay in the air."

Encountering thousands of turkeys in midair, Marine One could not fly. The copter's rotors chopped and smashed turkeys, but in turn, the rotors slowed. Additionally, turkeys smashed into the windshield like twenty-pound feathered raindrops, obscuring the pilot's view. Marine One crash-landed on the L, the famous elevated railroad track looping through downtown Chicago.

The violent landing stunned the First Family, although they and the Secret Service agents remained securely strapped in their seats and unharmed. Sensing a kill, thousands of zombie turkeys surrounded them.

"Gobble! Gobble!" That dreaded high-pitched cry echoed through Chicago's canyons.

At that moment, Sam and Lisa pulled up in their car, in the midst of the chaos of a hundred thousand turkeys in downtown Chicago, a feathered blizzard of death. Sam saw the helicopter crash, and since he was driving, Lisa caught it on video. She had acquired video cameras while they were in Joliet. Sam also pulled out his video camera and streamed the attack online. The zombie turkeys swarmed over the crippled copter like ants over a sugar cube. Then he recognized the helicopter.

"That's Marine One! The president's copter!"

"Oh, we've got to do something! Quick, Sam, drive closer! I've got an idea!"

Sam set the video camera into its mount on the dashboard. He drove under the tracks, beneath the helicopter. Zombie turkeys quickly surrounded the car.

"Gobble! Gobble!"

"Now what, Lisa?"

"This!" Lisa cracked the window and shot out flame from their flamethrower. "Eat flame and die, you turkeys!" The zombie turkeys scattered in panic.

"Spin the car around!" she cried. A circle of flame erupted from around their car.

"Don't spray around the helicopter! They might be leaking fuel," Sam warned.

Too late. The dripping aviation fuel fed the fire below, causing flames to leap upward to the tracks and to the helicopter. The Secret Service Agents in the copter dispatched the remaining zombie turkeys around them with deadly shooting from the doors. The turkeys scattered from the flames. The agents guided the presidential family from the endangered helicopter onto the L's tracks and away from the flames.

"Whew! That was a close one." The president sighed.

"Here comes the L!" shouted a Secret Service agent. "Get everyone off the tracks!"

Fortunately, part of the Secret Service agents' training included escape from an elevated railway. The six agents made a human chain from the tracks to the street, and the Obama family climbed down the agents' backs.

The train, surprisingly, did not slow down or brake. The operator and passengers had already been killed by hundreds of zombie turkeys, who piled into the cars at the last station. The train crashed into the helicopter with a fiery explosion of aviation fuel, baking the turkeys inside the train like a Thanksgiving oven. The flaming cars, now derailed, fell off the L, crashing to the street in a crazy, flaming jumble of death.

"Wow," Sam said. "I wonder how long turkeys have to cook at *that* temperature to be ready to eat?"

Sam and Lisa captured the flaming crash of the L into the presidential copter, the rescue of the presidential family, and their descent from the L on video, and live-streamed to the internet on the *Midley Beacon* website. After setting the dash camera to record the flaming L train, they went over to the agents and the First Family, standing next to the roasted and mashed turkeys below the L.

"Can we help?" Lisa asked.

The agent toggled his headset to Off. "Yes, we need to get the First Family safely to Grant Park. We've arranged a backup helicopter to pick them up there."

"Hop in, Mr., Mrs. Obama, Malia, Sasha," Sam said. Two agents went with them in the car, and four rode in the open trunk.

"I'm glad I've got this big old car," Sam said.

"I love these classic autos," Mr. Obama remarked.

"I'm glad you had that flamethrower!" Mrs. Obama said to Lisa.

"But it almost cooked our goose!" Sasha said.

"It's meant to cook the turkeys' goose." Lisa laughed.

"We got away from the helicopter just in time!" Malia said.

"And then we saw the train!" Sasha said. "We had to climb down the agents' backs."

"That's what they're there for," Mrs. Obama said.

The agents in the trunk provided covering fire with their pistols, suppressing turkey attacks on the car. Sam, using his usual heavy foot, squashed his normal share of slow and inattentive zombie turkeys wandering across the road. *Why did the turkey cross the road?* he thought. *Because it was a zombie.* He chuckled at his stupid joke.

"OK, Sam, turn right here at the Bean!" Lisa chimed in helpfully. The Bean, a mirrored sculpture, was a well-known Chicago landmark.

"I know how to get to Grant Park, Lisa."

Once they got to Grant Park, they drove to the second marine helicopter, idling near the Art Institute of Chicago.

"Thanks for giving us a lift!" the president said as he got out.

"And for saving our bacon," Mrs. Obama added.

"Although you almost burned us up!" Malia chimed in.

Lisa gave her and Sam's business cards, with the *Midley Beacon* website, to the president and First Lady and their children. "Be sure you see your video on the web!" she urged.

"We're on the *Midley Beacon* website! We're famous!" Sasha said.

"We go there every day for the latest zombie turkey video," Malia said.

"Say," Lisa said. "Could I record your endorsement of our paper?"

"Sure!"

Lisa quickly recorded their enthusiastic praise of the *Midley Beacon.* This was probably worth another $100,000 worth of web traffic, if not a million.

The marine copter lifted off with the presidential family and the agents. While Sam waved good-bye, Lisa scanned the sky and surroundings with her binoculars. She saw no turkeys; the downtown streets and skies were now deserted. Then she noticed turkeys along the lakefront.

"Hey, Sam. Let's head that way. I smell a story." The flock was only a short distance away—at the Shedd Aquarium. For some reason, hundreds of turkeys were scrambling to get in. Furthermore, through the aquarium's windows, Lisa saw hundreds more were already inside.

"Wow. That looks pretty dangerous," Sam said.

"Nothing a flamethrower won't clear up!"

"What if there are people in there?"

"Hmmm." Lisa remembered her near immolation of the president's helicopter. "Maybe we should look first, flame later. Drive around the building. See if there is another way in."

Driving around the building, Sam squashed a few turkeys, but most of them crowded by the broken front door. He saw a door ajar behind the facility. No turkeys were on that side. Pulling up with squealing tires, they got out and peeked around the door. It seemed to be a fire escape door, leading to a stairway. Faint sounds of gobbling echoed down the stairwell.

"I assume this door being ajar means the people inside got away," Lisa commented.

"I hope you're right. I've got a bad feeling about this whole situation."

They went up the stairs. As they climbed higher, the gobbling grew louder.

"Gobble! Gobble! Gobble! Gobble! Gobble! Gobble! Gobble! Gobble! Gobble! Gobble! *GOBBLE! GOBBLE!*"

"Something about that last 'gobble, gobble' doesn't sound right," Sam said.

They cautiously looked in the topmost door, which opened onto a platform looking down on a large pool full of sea creatures—including a great white shark. A man at the edge of the pool blew a turkey call. *GOBBLE! GOBBLE!* That explained the odd sound Sam had heard.

The zombie turkeys responded with "Gobble! Gobble!" and advanced en masse on the man, surrounding him. They seemed mesmerized by the call, staring with red eyes but quietly marching forward. The man wore a khaki, camouflaged hunting outfit, camo boots, and a full, bushy beard.

Sam called to him, "Hey, you! You can escape this way!"

He looked at them, "Yeah, I know. I've got to kill these buggers."

"How will you kill them with a turkey caller?"

"By getting them into the pool with me. It's salt water. I've already gone through my ammo!" He jumped into the aquarium tank.

"Noo!" Lisa gasped.

From the water he called, *GOBBLE! GOBBLE!* Like lemmings, the massed turkeys moved forward, plopping into the water like feathered, twenty-pound Alka-Seltzer tablets. The ones behind pressed the others forward. Soon, hundreds upon hundreds of turkeys covered the surface of the water, like a turkey-patterned pool cover.

As soon as they were in the salt water, the zombie turkeys lost their red eyes. They swam as well as turkeys normally do—badly.

Then the great white shark hit. Gobbling the turkeys three and four at a time, the shark seemed delighted by this extra feeding. *This food is so fresh and crunchy!*

The shark was an automatic eating machine: bite, crunch, swallow...bite crunch, swallow...

"Get out of there!" Sam called. The man continued to issue the turkey call *GOBBLE! GOBBLE!* until the last of the turkeys plopped in. Then he swam for the exit ladder.

His swimming motion attracted the shark. Bite, crunch, swallow. *That bite tasted different.* Bite, crunch, swallow. *So did that one.* The man disappeared under the water.

"Oh, Sam. That was horrible," Lisa said as they averted their eyes from the now bloody pool.

"Yet there is no greater love than to give your life for your fellow man. He single-handedly killed hundreds of turkeys."

"At least I got his sacrifice on streaming video. Maybe he can be identified."

Lisa pointed to the lakefront windows of the upper story of the Shedd Aquarium. "Let's reconnoiter from here." No flocks were visible southward, toward Soldier Field. Military choppers and airplanes were everywhere. Over the Loop area there were random dots of flocks of turkeys, but not more than a couple hundred. Looking north, they stopped. A mass of turkeys crowded around the Navy Pier amusement park.

"Navy Pier next, Lisa?" Sam queried.

"Yup. Someone's gotta do it. Might as well be us." They ran back down the fire escape. "We've got enough material to maintain our web traffic for the next two weeks. This additional story might give us another week."

Chapter 10

Navy Pier

On their way over to Navy Pier, Lisa checked on the other reporters. They had filed online reports from their unique perspectives. Charlie Gomez covered the battle of Soldier field, in gory detail, right down to the celebratory singing of "Over the River and through the Wood." He also added the detail that the Thanksgiving Day game had the highest ratings of any NFL game in history—and football hadn't even been played.

President Obama, now safely on Air Force One with his family, held a nationwide broadcast from the airplane, recognizing the sacrifices of the US soldiers and civilians fighting the zombies. He specifically mentioned how the Packers and Bears fans had cooperated, and how the Republicans and Democrats should too. He also personally thanked Lisa Kambacher and Sam Melvin of the *Midley Beacon*.

"Crap! He got my name wrong. Double crap! It's wrong on my business cards," Lisa cried.

"It's only been a few days since we were married," Sam said soothingly.

"I could've had them reprinted by now!" Lisa growled.

Sam smiled. She sounded like her old self.

Lisa next called Serena Fields, who covered the second battle of Princeville. More zombie turkeys attacked the second time, but the prepared townspeople had repulsed the turkeys with great success. Everyone in town had a supply of Molotov cocktails, and quite a few had flamethrowers. Warren

Zapp led a group of local militia to finish wiping them out. Mop-up operations continued with tracking dogs.

Bret Brown reported from Bartonville and Peoria. The zombie turkeys had attacked West Peoria but had been defeated by the local anti-zombie militia. Caterpillar had also helped out. The Edwards training center donated tanker trucks that went up and down the streets, spraying salt water on the zombies and turning them into normal turkeys. The local militia then harvested the flock for Thanksgiving. The homeless missions and poor people within Peoria had plenty of turkeys.

In Joliet, Sarah Phillips and Rob Peterson reported the successful destruction of turkeys throughout the town. Roving bands of citizen hunters armed with shotguns and flamethrowers effectively stopped the zombie turkey incursion. The Chicago gangs and the NRA gun clubs united in hunting the zombies. Unarmed civilians stayed home in their homes. After clearing the zombie turkeys out to the city limits, the hunters used dogs to track down the stragglers and find their hibernation locations.

A large flock had blocked I-80, which ran through Joliet. The Illinois Department of Transportation had sent snow plows to clear them off. Rather than running from the oncoming plows, the turkeys actually flew into them, apparently believing they could peck them to pieces. The turkeys cracked several windshields, but came out on the short end of that collision. After piling the stunned and dead turkeys into long windrows beside I-80, the Joliet militia finished them off with flamethrowers.

In Tinley Park, Lashon Bigelow reported the details about the successful military operation that had driven the turkeys out over the lake. Fléchette weapons and salt water tankers bombing masses of turkeys on the ground had done the job. The military groups then realized the flock they had defeated had flown across the lake to Chicago. The planes, copters, and soldiers followed them and drove the turkeys north and east toward the lake.

Lashon followed the military to Chicago and then reported on serious injuries of people in Chicago supermarkets. At every grocery store loaded with fresh turkeys for Thanksgiving, hundreds had resurrected overnight and attacked store personnel, who opened up the stores the next morning. The National Guard went from store to store wiping the zombies out, but hundreds and thousands joined the other flocks of zombie turkeys. Thanksgiving Day shoppers faced a turkey shortage.

However, the citizens of Chicago remedied the shortage by organizing into hunting groups. They shot and slaughtered the turkeys and then delivered the carcasses to the poor for Thanksgiving. Some were already cooked. One enterprising hunter published a recipe for how to roast a zombie turkey for Thanksgiving using a flamethrower. Lashon linked that to the *Midley Beacon* newspaper website. Meanwhile, clouds of smoke from flamethrowers in use around the town rose up in columns all over the city.

Lashon had gone from the grocery stores in the suburbs to the Loop, following the flocks. In the Loop she saw Chicago city employees use city snowplows, all primed and ready for winter, to clear the streets of the Loop. Two or more snowplows would drive side by side down the streets, piling the turkeys into huge clumps and throwing them to the side. Then National Guard soldiers with fléchette rockets, or Humvees with fléchette cannons, would shred the stunned, dazed, and sometimes dead turkey clumps into nonresurrectable turkey sauce.

Lashon's phone chimed. Caller ID showed *Lisa*.

"Good job, Lashon!"

"Thanks, Lisa. Reporting for the *Midley Beacon* is sure more interesting than the police and coroner's beat in Gary, Indiana."

"Didn't I tell you that? We're heading toward Navy Pier. There are still a few loose ends to our reporting at Shedd Aquarium. See if you can find out who that guy was that sacrificed himself to kill those turkeys. See if you can document his backstory."

"Will do. I'm headed there now." Lashon left the Chicago Loop and headed for Shedd Aquarium. She was very familiar with Chicago, having visited it since she was a girl growing up in Gary. She had played basketball there, gone to sports events there, and had even gone on a few dates there. She grimaced. Those hadn't worked out. She'd rather deal with zombie turkeys than those guys.

* * *

"Quick! Turn off the ovens and the fryers! Everyone get to the bomb shelter!" Betty shouted as the klaxon continued to ring. One of her improvements on the farm since Tom's death had been to link all the turkey traps around the perimeter to a home alarm.

The bomb shelter was off the basement rec room. Helen directed everyone, while Betty turned off the ovens and burners, and Hank ran outside and turned off the fryer in the driveway in front of the garage. Too bad—the thermometer showed the oil to be 375 degrees, just right for frying.

"Gobble! Gobble!"

A dozen turkeys rushed him. Hank threw the four-gallon pot of oil at the lead turkey and delightedly heard *Ssssz!* as the turkey fried alive. Grabbing a tank of gas by the lawnmower, he threw the gas over the oil and then ignited it with the spark igniter for the fryer. The onrushing turkeys were just a few feet away, ignoring their suffering leader writhing on the ground.

Whoom! The gas exploded, and then the oil on the gravel driveway flared up. The turkeys burst into flame like cotton balls on a gas grill.

"Gobble! Gobble!" The main flock of perhaps a thousand turkeys landed only a hundred feet away. Hank rushed into the house and down into the bomb shelter.

Betty waited for him at the door. "I saw what you did there. Well done. Tom couldn't have done any better."

Suddenly, Hank's eyes were moist. High praise indeed.

"Did you get something in your eye?" Betty asked with concern.

"Yeah, it's nothing. Probably just the gas fumes."

"OK. Listen to them out there!" The turkeys attacked the house furiously. "My insurance agent won't like another claim. He'll probably raise my rates again."

They watched the ravening zombie turkeys peck the windows and doors, via the multiple screens in the shelter, fed by the security cameras.

"We need to lure them away from the house before they get in here," Hank said.

"Hmmm. We have Tom's beekeeper suit down here..." Betty mused. "It's too big for me. But if one of you men were willing, you could go to the barn and activate the apocalypse trap."

"I'll do it!" Hank said.

Caleb Yoder, Helen's son, said, "I'd do it if I had to, but I'd rather not." He looked at his wife and children, who were looking at him big eyed.

"Dad! Don't leave us!" Lauren Williams cried.

"We've already lost Mom. We don't want to lose you!" Ryan exclaimed.

"Will you be safe in that thing?" Rachel asked.

"You be the judge," Betty said. She showed them the suit. Tom had reinforced it with sheet metal, duct taped around the arms, legs, torso, and head. A scratched Plexiglas visor came down over the face like a knight's helmet.

"Kids, I have to do this for Mom. This'll be revenge," Hank said savagely.

Hank tried it on. It fit badly, for he was several inches taller than Tom. He could live with it, except for the gaps at the neck and the wrists. Betty duct-taped the gaps, layering the duct tape with pieces of aluminum cut from baking pans she had stored in the room.

Hank noticed the ominous reddish-brown stain inside the helmet. Tom's blood. "I'll get them for you, Tom."

"Thank you, Hank." Betty said fervently.

Hank started. He hadn't realized he had spoken aloud.

"Hank, the knife switch for the trap is in Tom's office in the barn, by the front door. We've kept the trap primed and ready in case of any new attack. The turkeys will attack you as soon as you step outside, so get inside as quickly as you can." Betty walked with him up the stairs to the outside exit.

A horizontal oak door lay between them and the killer turkeys.

"Get back in the bomb shelter, Betty."

"I've got to do this before you go." She kissed him on the visor. "That's for luck."

His heart was curiously light as he lifted the heavy door and waded into the stream of maddened zombie turkeys. Betty had said to hurry to the barn, and he had intended to run, but he could barely walk. Buffeted by turkeys crashing into him, with their spurs and beaks hitting him like trip hammers, he ploughed his way to the barn. One good thing about the crazed flock—he was luring them away from the house and toward the barn. All of the thousand turkeys followed him.

He saw why the visor was scratched; turkey spurs added dozens of new gouges to the tough Plexiglas. He opened the door to Tom's office and tried to shut it. He had to kick aggressive turkeys out of the way, and as he slammed the heavy door, a couple turkey heads dropped to the floor.

"Whew!" Hank started to remove the hot helmet and then stopped. He remembered how Tom had died. He saw the knife switch. "Here goes!"

The lights dimmed as dozens of servo motors went on, moving the trench covers up and toward the barn. The heavy metal covers protected the base of the barn from the flame. Turkeys pushed into the trenches, in their frenzy to get to Hank. Betty had expanded the trenches to completely encircle the barn. She'd also added twice as much gasoline as Tom had used. She *really* wanted those turkeys dead.

The lights dimmed again as the sparkers flashed the gasoline into ferocious flame. Hundreds of turkeys were instantly immolated. Others, splashed with gasoline, ran about, incinerating their fellow gasoline-soaked turkeys.

The lights dimmed a third and final time. Betty had added a new feature: a pumping system that sprayed gasoline away from the barn into the surrounding yard. A solid sheet of fire covered the remaining turkeys like a blanket from hell.

* * *

Zombie turkeys packed Navy Pier. No people were visible at all. Sam drove the big Lincoln at high speed to the middle of the pier. The turkeys splashed and splattered off and under his car, but he knew how to drive on turkey guts by now. The turkeys were most crowded around the entrance to the Shakespearean Theatre.

"OK, let's go in there," Lisa said.

"Flamethrower?"

"Of course." Once more Lisa shot the flamethrower while Sam drove the car around in a circle. After the few minutes of turkey flambé, the zombies scattered from that entrance.

Inside, they found out what had happened. Several hundred turkeys had entered the theater, pecking and kicking actors and audience alike. Then the tables had turned. The theater audience, like the football crowd, had come armed with knives. The actors also snatched weapons out of the prop case and attacked the turkeys with halberds, knives, spears, and swords.

The powerful turkeys had broken one of the windows, and the crowd took turns holding off the swarm, when Sam and Lisa arrived and cleared them away. Soon afterward, the turkeys returned and began to press in again.

"Gobble! Gobble!"

"Don't worry. I've got a flamethrower," Lisa said. "Eat flame, you turkeys!" She shot a flame of about four feet, and it gave out. No more napalm. "Oops. Do we have more napalm in the car?" she asked Sam.

"Yeah. Don't leave home without it—but—look!" Thousands of the creatures wedged in between them and the car.

"I guess we can hold off the turkeys with the people we have here—" Another window broke behind them. Hundreds of more zombie turkeys flooded in, feathery death, pecking and kicking any who got in their way.

"Oh no!" Unarmed, Lisa quickly abandoned the flamethrower and ran upstairs. Sam followed her, providing rear-guard protection. The armed members of the audience and the actors held off the turkeys on the stairs to the upper floors, while the unarmed hid upstairs. But turkeys began flying up and attacking. Sam used his pistol—until he ran out of ammo. Lisa used a switchblade she kept in her purse, to split the shot turkeys.

"You're pretty good with that."

"You don't go through thirty-three Thanksgivings without learning how to carve a turkey!"

More and more turkeys landed upstairs. People fled into the theater again, closing the doors.

"It looks like those buggers will finally get us, Sam."

"I won't go down without a fight!" He savagely wrung the head off a turkey. Lisa then split the turkey with her switchblade, describing how to do it while Sam video-streamed the process online.

"It's really getting cold in here with the windows broken." Sam consulted the weather app on his phone. "It's a blizzard! A blizzard is hitting right now!"

The temperature dropped below freezing inside the building. Outside, it fell below zero. The wind howled and whistled through the broken windows. The turkeys in the building stopped attacking and ran about like chickens with their heads cut off, looking for shelter. This allowed the audience and the actors with weapons to counterattack and hack them to pieces.

Outside, thousands of turkeys huddled together against the lee of the building. Then a military tanker dumped a load of salt water on them. In the forty-mile-per-hour wind, they quickly froze.

"Brined turkey!" Lisa said brightly.

"They're freezing out there."

"We're freezing in here! I can hardly hold the video camera."

The army followed up the airborne assault. Hundreds of soldiers formed up in ranks, and fixed bayonets. "Charge!" The soldiers ran up and down the roads and sidewalks of Navy Pier, skewering half-frozen turkeys. Fleeing from these deadly, bladed predators, a huge group of turkeys fell into the lake. Some froze in place, and others froze in midair, dropping to the ground like giant hailstones. Lisa videoed the last zombie turkey remnant, flying south along the lakefront, directly toward the army's field headquarters. A vertical hail of fléchettes brought most down. A few stragglers flew on.

* * *

He felt great—but he was cold. He led his hens out of the freezing wind toward one of the tunnels that went under Lakeshore Drive. He could barely fly in the strong wind, and he lost one hen after another to the cold. Finally, there was just him. A squall blew furiously, driving heavy snow as well. He knew if he got into the tunnel, he'd be all right.

He landed and tumbled over, blown by the wind. He tried to walk and couldn't. So tired. He wasn't cold any more. The snow began to cover him. So sleepy. Instinctively, he called for help.

"Gobble. Gobble."

The wind howled in reply.

* * *

The other homeless guys called him Moses because he was old and had a patriarchal white beard. He rubbed his hands gratefully over the fifty-five-gallon drum filled with blazing scrap wood, which he had placed in the tunnel to keep him warm in this terrible blizzard. It wasn't easy being homeless in Chicago in the winter. Many homeless used these tunnels under Lakeshore Drive. He had blocked the entrance to the tunnel with a four-by-eight piece of plywood, braced with a box of wood and another fifty-five-gallon drum containing more scrap wood. The smoke from the fire was sucked out of the tunnel by the wind. As Moses arranged this barricade, he saw the big tom turkey just outside the tunnel. Huddling in his parka he had gotten from the Salvation Army, Moses went outside and picked it up. It was a big one, maybe twenty-five pounds, and just about frozen. And he was hungry. Great! Turkey dinner for Thanksgiving! He had some aluminum foil and an old pot. He could roast it over his fire.

"Gobble, gobble," he said as he started to butcher the turkey in the tunnel.

Chapter 11

Shedd Aquarium

Lashon Bigelow arrived at the Shedd Aquarium amid a howling blizzard. Any outward sign of the turkeys had been covered. The military, having wiped out the turkeys, had moved on, looking elsewhere for the zombies. However, the doors to the aquarium were ajar, a sure sign of forced entry by zombie turkeys.

Lashon had jumped at the chance to become an e-reporter for the *Midley Beacon* when Lisa had called her last week. The pay was no better than at the Gary, Indiana, paper, but Lisa had promised her a portion of the advertising from YouTube and the newspaper site, based upon the traffic for her stories. Any improvement was good, and Lisa said the bonuses could amount to thousands of dollars. Lashon was working her way through online journalism school, and she just needed three more courses to get her BA.

What a mess! Shredded and chopped turkeys covered the inside of the aquarium. She counted 153, give or take a half a turkey, as she methodically surveyed each floor of the aquarium. Turkey droppings and feathers covered the top observation deck for the salt water tank. A ghastly soup of turkey parts and feathers filled the tank itself. She prepared herself for the worst regarding the unknown man who had jumped in, but she was not prepared for what she saw.

A man had climbed the ladder out of the tank and lay motionless next to it. Impressive, considering his left leg was gone below the knee and his right foot ended in a stump at the ankle. Lashon ran to him and checked his heartbeat and breathing. She trained in CPR and first aid in high school and knew how to revive him. His heart beat rapidly, and his breathing was shallow. She dialed 911 on her phone for the ambulance. Meanwhile, she dressed his stumps. He was cold and wet. She put her coat over him and went downstairs and closed the doors. She hoped the building would heat up now that the doors were closed. Still, he was cold and probably in shock. She dragged him from the cold tank room to an office. It was a good thing she was a big woman. She'd played center on her high school basketball team. He was a large man and heavier than he looked.

Once in the office, Lashon took the curtains down and wrapped him in them. She checked him again. Still in shock. The ambulance probably wouldn't be here in time.

She sighed. She knew what she had to do. She unwrapped him and crawled in next to him and then wrapped them both in the curtains. She was really going above and beyond to get the story. She studied his face carefully. He wasn't as ugly as he first appeared. The big, bushy beard hid his square jaw, which matched his broad, square face—which went with his square, muscular frame. He didn't smell bad either, once you got past the smell of the fish tank.

Her instinctive reaction to his camo getup and hunting gear was that he was just a typical redneck cracker out hunting turkeys. Of course, how many crackers did a girl from the Gary ghetto really know? All she knew were the caricatures from TV and movies—and she knew how inaccurate they were about black people. She remembered her grandmother telling her, "White folks is jes' folks, like black folks is jes' folks." Her grandmother had grown up in southern Alabama, where whites and blacks got along, as long as blacks didn't get "uppity." Her grandmother had taught her tolerance and love for all races, and she didn't have any grudge against white folks, despite the discrimination she had suffered.

Lashon shivered. His cold body sucked heat from her, even though she was very warm blooded. She hoped he was warming up. His breathing seemed deeper and smoother. She checked his pulse. Slow and regular. Good. As she wriggled to get comfortable, she felt something long and hard by his leg. Feeling carefully, she pulled out a huge knife. The blade alone was twelve inches long, with another five inches for the handle.

"Woo-wee!" She whistled, peering at it closely. There were spots of blood on the leather-wrapped handle. "This would split a turkey jes' fine. I wonder if he used it on the shark?"

The man gave a sigh. He was warming up. Slowly he opened his eyes. Unfocused gray eyes looked sightlessly at her. Then his brows furrowed.

"Who are you?"

"Lashon Bigelow."

He seemed to be thinking deeply.

"Are you an angel? When the shark bit me, I thought I was a goner."

Lashon chuckled. She had never been called an angel before. "You almost were a goner. I didn't expect to find you alive when I came here. You almost died. If I had been fifteen minutes later, you'd be gone."

"How did I get here? I vaguely recall climbing out of the tank. It hurt so much. It shouldn't have been that hard."

"Yeah, I can see that." She didn't want to tell him he'd lost both his feet. She couldn't imagine climbing a ladder with two stumps. "I found you lying at the top of the tank, half-frozen to death. I moved you in here and wrapped you up, but you were still in shock, and freezing. So I had to warm you up myself."

"Fine job you're doing too. I'm very comfortable, on the side toward you. My legs hurt like hell though. Do I have anything left to my feet?"

"I'm sorry, no."

"Yeah. I thought so. I saw him take my left leg, and I had to wriggle like hell to get away. I was just starting up the ladder when he got my right foot. I must have passed out soon after that."

"I found this on you." She showed him the big knife. "I figured you used it on the turkeys and maybe the shark."

"Yeah, I used it to split the turkeys I killed, when I had a chance. I didn't use it on the shark—it all happened so fast."

"I'm impressed you're alive and how you rescued yourself. Could you tell me the whole story?"

"Sure, it's the least I can do for the lady who saved my life."

"Oh, and could you tell me your name?" His admiration for her embarrassed her.

"Rulon Miller. Well, when I heard the zombie turkeys were here in Chicago..." Rulon related his preparations and packing.

Lashon was quite interested and asked many questions about his weapons, his truck, and his turkey calls.

"Then I left and came north, looking for turkeys."

"Where did you first see them?"

"I saw a few scattered turkeys here and there, none worth hunting. I listened to the radio and heard about the attacks at Soldier Field. When I got there, the military had cordoned off the area. I followed stray flocks to the lakefront near the Shedd Aquarium. There I got out my trusty turkey call." He pulled it out of his vest pocket. *GOBBLE! GOBBLE!*

Lashon jumped. "Oh! I didn't expect it to be so loud!"

"Sorry. It's loud, and it attracts all kinds of turkeys, hens and toms. I made it myself," he added proudly. "Anyway, it attracted a *lot* of turkeys. I shot a bunch of them, but they were coming faster than I could kill them."

"What did you do?"

"I saw the Shedd Aquarium was nearby, so I marched, like the Pied Piper of turkeys, gobbling all the way. At first I thought I would just kill them when they were bunched outside the door, but then I thought, 'Hey, they're stopped by salt water. There's a salt water tank here. Let me lead them there.' So I did. I followed the signs to the salt water tanks and then upstairs to the opening. Then I was stuck. I had hundreds of murderous zombie turkeys behind me. How could I get them into the tank? The only way I thought of was to jump in and call them in!"

"Didn't you worry about the white shark?"

"Yeah, a little. I figured he'd be too busy eating turkey to get me. I was almost right—off by two feet."

Lashon chuckled uncertainly. He seemed like a normal, garrulous guy—but she wasn't used to people joking about being a double amputee.

"So what about you? How did you get here just when I needed you?"

"I'm an e-reporter for the *Midley Beacon*. My editor asked me to come here and get the details about the guy who sacrificed himself to kill the turkeys."

"Great! I love that news site! That's where I get all my zombie turkey news."

"Did you see two reporters there when you jumped in?"

"Were those reporters? All I remember was that they tried to talk me out of jumping. I kind of lost track of them, fighting a shark and everything."

"That was my boss, Lisa Melvin, and the head investigative reporter, Sam Melvin. They just got married before the attack on Joliet."

"*The* Lisa and Sam? The ace zombie turkey reporters?"

"The very same."

"This is the first time I've been famous! Will this make the *Midley Beacon* website?"

"For sure."

Just then they heard the ambulance siren coming in the distance.

"Ah. The EMTs should be able to help you. Let me go and lead the EMTs to you." She unwrapped them and then wrapped Rulon up again.

"It's a lot chillier without you, Rashon."

"That's 'Lashon.' The EMTs will be here in a minute." She ran down the stairs, met them at the door, and led them up to Rulon. They removed the wet curtains, his wet clothing, wrapped him in a blanket, gave him an IV, and checked her bandages. They rewrapped his stumps, doing a neater job than she had.

"I'll miss you, Rashon," Rulon said as they carried him to the elevator.

"That's 'Lashon.'"

"Sorry." He looked downcast.

"I'll visit you in the hospital!" she promised.

"I'll look forward to that." He brightened, and a smile split his beard before the ambulance doors closed.

I will look forward to seeing you too. I don't even know if he's single! she thought. She wrote up the story, added the video she had taken at the aquarium, and uploaded it to the YouTube channel. She also called Lisa and give her a verbal report.

"So what's this Rulon Miller like as a person?"

"He looks a like a redneck, a friendly redneck that just walked off the set of *Duck Dynasty*."

"Weren't you grossed out by his bleeding leg stumps?"

"Nah. I was a nurses' aid as a teenager, and I saw plenty of grosser things than that."

"So you wrapped his stumps up and then what?"

"I wrapped him in a curtain in a warm room. He still didn't get warm enough to live, so I crawled next to him to warm him up."

"Was it sexy?"

"I don't even know him! It was cold and wet, and it worked." Lashon's irritation came through.

"Sorry, Lashon. I didn't mean to get personal. I was just joking. How long was it before the EMTs came?"

"About half an hour."

"Be sure to write up the story and upload it tonight, along with all your video."

"I already did that. I also completed all my reports on the Chicago supermarkets and the neighborhood battles, as well as the battle at Tinley Park."

"Great! See you."

When she visited Rulon in the hospital the next day, Lashon found out he was single.

Rulon enjoyed seeing his story on the *Midley Beacon* website.

Lashon also delighted in reading Lisa's story about her saving Rulon's life. She had not written that up, nor would she have written it up the way Lisa did, making her out to be a hero, but Lisa did, based upon their phone conversation. It sounded heroic, but she just did basic first aid, as she had been taught.

"Your story is a big hit on the internet, Rulon," Lashon said.

"Gee, that's great. How about your story?"

"Oh, you read that too?"

"I read everything on the *Midley Beacon* website. I'd buy the T-shirt, if they sold them."

Lashon made a mental note to sell *Midley Beacon* T-shirts on the website. Lisa would surely go for that. "It embarrassed me a little. It made me sound like such a hero."

"You were! You saved my life! That's what a hero does!"

"Anyway, I'd like your permission to conduct a video interview from the hospital bed. People want a blow-by-blow description of how you defeated the zombie turkeys in Shedd Aquarium."

"Sure thing!"

Lashon started the video camera and led him through his story, from the time he started packing his weapons, the making of his turkey calls, and his last thoughts as he struggled up the ladder. Lashon added her portion, turning the camera on herself: finding him, administering first aid, calling 911, staying with him until the ambulance arrived. She mentioned she dried him off and wrapped him in curtains, but glossed over the fact she warmed him with her own body. Rulon didn't let that slide.

"Hey, Lashon! You forgot something." She turned the camera to him, expecting him to add something about the ambulance ride.

"You left off the fact you warmed me with your own body until the ambulance came and delivered me from shock."

"Well, yeah."

"Let me have that camera." She gave it to him. He interviewed her. "What did you think when you first saw Rulon?"

She went with it. They could always edit it later.

"I checked your vitals. You were in shock: shallow breathing, rapid heartbeat, very cold."

"How cold was I?"

"I didn't have a thermometer, but you were below normal body temperature. The room was open to the outside, perhaps fifty degrees, and the water was warmer, maybe eighty degrees."

"Where was I?"

"Flat on the ground, bleeding into the pool"

"What did you do?"

"I bandaged your legs with towels and then dragged you into a warmer office. I took the drapes down and wrapped you up. When you didn't get warmer, I wrapped both of us up in the drapes. I also called the ambulance."

Rulon's grin split his beard. "How long were we wrapped together?"

"Maybe half an hour."

"When did I wake up?"

"Five minutes before the ambulance came."

Rulon turned the camera on himself. "That's it, *Midley Beacon* viewers. Straight from the heroine of Shedd Aquarium. This is Rulon Miller saying good night and God bless."

"What a ham!"

The nurse came in. "Visiting hour is over, Ms. Bigelow."

"Will you visit me tomorrow?"

"Sure."

"See you on the web!"

* * *

The combined Rulon Miller and Lashon Bigelow interview drew millions of views on YouTube. Lisa grinned from ear to ear the next day as she handed Lashon a bonus check based upon the hits and the advertising revenue. Now that the *Midley Beacon* had a big, steady cash flow, Lisa had changed from a nasty pinchpenny to giving out bonus checks to her employees whenever their stories reached a certain level of popularity.

This practice attracted many eager reporters and bloggers from around the country, seeking to work for the prestigious *Midley Beacon*. Lisa and Sam interviewed them at first, with Lisa interviewing the bloggers and Sam the reporters, but the flood of applications overwhelmed them. Lisa hired an HR specialist, Karen Mooney, and trained her in what they wanted in bloggers and reporters.

"Divide the applicants into the Nos and the Maybes. Turn down the Nos and send us the Maybes." That got rid of most of the applicants.

Karen's well worth the money we pay her, Lisa said to herself.

Lisa also signed a contract with a T-shirt manufacturer in Peoria to print *Midley Beacon* T-shirts with pictures of each reporter on the front and a zombie turkey on the back. They proved to be so popular that Lisa also added a line of hoodies, coffee mugs, coasters, and insulated cups, also emblazoned with various reporters faces.

* * *

At the Indian Turkey Farm, a hundred thousand red-eyed zombie turkeys burst from their pens and savaged the farmworkers. Aaron Root fled to the receiving office and locked the door.

"Gobble! Gobble!" They pecked and scratched incessantly on the door.

He called 911.

"Help! This is the Indian Turkey Farm! Our turkeys have gone zombie! I'm the only one left alive!"

"You just stay right where you are. We'll send someone over right away."

"It'd better be a lot of someones, and they'd better come quickly! I don't know how long this door will last!"

"We'll send someone as quickly as we can!"

"Hurry! This is just a hollow-core door! They're already halfway through!"

"I'm sorry. I couldn't understand you. What did you—" The phone went dead. His battery had died.

The first turkey's beak went through the door. Then a spur. Then hundreds of others. Then thousands. They flooded into the room.

"Gobble! Gobble!"

Later, they took off looking for more food.

Chapter 12

Turkey Institute

The Turkey Institute had been busy ever since the first zombie turkeys had arrived. They pursued multiple paths of investigation. First, an antibiotic. Salt water worked great after the fact, but they wanted a preventative treatment that would protect the country's turkey flocks from the danger. They'd made some progress; the old sulfa drugs that had been used in World War I, before penicillin had been invented, proved partially effective. The institute worked on improving the drug's effectiveness.

Secondly, the institute researched how the bacteria copied the DNA from various cells and actually transformed into another cell. Dr. Galloway personally led this research. This bacterium extracted the cellular DNA and then replaced its own DNA with the cell's DNA. The new cell perfectly replicated normal tissue but reproduced as fast as bacteria could, doubling in quantity every twenty minutes. Dr. Galloway had a video of a turkey leg growing back, after he amputated it, in thirty minutes. He planned to use that in his paper on the bacteria. Maybe he would get a Nobel Prize.

Thirdly, they researched the origin of this mutated bacteria. Members of the Turkey Institute scoured the area where the first zombie turkeys had appeared, in a forested area near the Illinois River, south of Bartonville. Superficially, the bacteria seemed to be a mutation of the common E. coli bacteria, found in the guts of humans and animals. Yet the cloning portion of its genetic code was unique. Where had that come from? Taking thousands of soil samples in a five-mile radius of the first attack, and then testing for the bacterium back in the labs, they found the bacterium randomly distributed through the woods, and not in farmers' fields—but in every sample in one particular field.

They contacted the farmer who owned that field. He had leased his field out to Corn-All, a national seed-corn grower. The farmer still had a few bags of seed corn he had sown there. Working closely with the National Center for Biotechnology Information Center, Dr. Galloway analyzed the genetic sequence of the corn. Fascinating! Corn-All apparently had an unpublished, secret genetic modification, designed to thwart ear rot and other corn diseases. The genetic modification would adapt to the disease at a cellular level and neutralize it by copying the DNA from the disease organism, whether fungal or bacteria.

"That's brilliant," Dr. Galloway murmured to himself. "I wonder if it matches the E. coli Gallopavo sequence?" (Dr Galloway had named the zombie turkey bacteria E. Coli Gallopavo. or Turkey E. coli, or ECG for short, in his seminal, yet-to-be-published paper.)

He ran the corn sample on the DNA sequencer and compared it to the bacterial DNA. The ECG DNA sequence that copied the cells' DNA matched exactly with the corn modified DNA.

Now, how did that DNA get from the corn to the bacteria? Dr. Galloway wondered. He directed his laboratory to feed the GM-modified corn to various animals, and then he tested their dung for the ECG bacteria. Pig: nothing. Chicken: nothing. Cow: nothing. Turkey: yes. In the turkey gut, the GMO corn combined with the normal E. coli, and a small amount of ECG was produced. The turkeys that ate the GMO corn did *not* turn zombie. Nor did turkeys eating ECG in any form. But an aerosol spray or an injection of ECG would cause them to turn.

Dr. Galloway had just finished writing up his findings when Sam and Lisa Melvin appeared at the Turkey Institute and asked for him.

* * *

Since they were in Chicago following up on zombie turkey stories, Lisa thought it would be good to see what new things the Turkey Institute had discovered about the disease.

After sitting in Dr. Galloway's office, Lisa said, "I'm curious about what you've learned about this zombie turkey disease since your last news conference."

"Quite a bit. First I wanted to know how this bacterium mutated the way it did. We took samples all around the original infection site in Bartonville and found it began in one field. We examined the seed used there, and it had been genetically modified to fight off corn disease. Those modifications were found in the turkey bacteria, E. coli Gallopavo, or ECG for short. That field grew corn for Corn-All, the seed company. I contacted Corn-All, and they confirmed they had made the modification."

"Wow," Sam said. "So GMO corn caused the zombie turkey virus!"

"Not directly. Rather, the corn combined with the E. coli in the guts of wild turkey, and *that's* what modified the bacterium. Then ECG bacterium had to be inhaled or get into the blood stream to cause the zombie disease."

"Is Corn-All liable for all the deaths and damage from the zombie turkeys?" Lisa asked.

"I'm not a lawyer, but I don't think so. They modified corn, not bacteria. Only by happenstance did that the corn get into the wild turkeys, and then by further random chance that the new bacteria caused the disease."

"Huh. What happened to that field of GMO corn?" Sam asked.

"Hmm. I didn't ask Corn-All that question. Let me get back to you on that."

The video of the turkey growing its leg back intrigued Lisa. "Dr. Galloway, could I post it to the *Midley Beacon* YouTube channel?"

"Sure. Here's a thumb drive with it. Be sure to credit the Turkey Institute."

"Now I've taken notes about the Corn-All connection. Here is the story I've written up while you were talking. Could I post this on the *Midley* site as well, or is this secret? Make allowances for the fact I'm just a layman and wrote it at that level," Lisa said.

"Shouldn't be a problem. The only secret is Corn-All's genetic modification, and I've only discovered what it is, not how they did it. Let's review the technical points for correctness."

After Dr. Galloway verified the story's accuracy, Lisa said, "This will be a bombshell, Dr. Galloway. Thanks for letting us publish it."

"Technically, it's just an announcement of findings. The formal publication will be peer reviewed in the next quarterly publication of the *Journal of Turkey Medicine*, JOTM. Make sure you mention that the paper is forthcoming."

"Consider it done.

"Huh. I've never heard of the *Journal of Turkey Medicine* before," Sam said.

"It's the most prestigious poultry medicine publication in the world. But not that many people are into poultry."

"Although poultry gets into many people," Sam said with a smile.

"And that's why poultry medicine is so important. I almost died from salmonella when I was a kid. That got me interested in poultry medicine."

"Interesting!" Lisa said. "Can I add that to the story?"

"Of course," Dr. Galloway said, smiling.

The *Midley Beacon*'s headline read "The Origin of the Zombie Turkeys" on its website, its YouTube channel, and its paper edition. The story covered the Corn-All GMO corn origin and the process that led to the turkey zombie bacterium.

Over 250,000 people subscribed to the paper edition of the *Midley Beacon*. About half of that circulation came from central Illinois, a hotbed of zombie turkey interest. The other half went around the nation and around world. Many people just liked paper copies of newspapers delivered to their homes daily. This still did not match the millions of *Midley Beacon* readers who went to the paper's website, nor the million-plus copies put on various e-readers as a magazine, nor the tens of millions of hits their YouTube channel got daily.

"We're over a hundred million hits on YouTube, Lisa," Sam said happily in their Chicago hotel room. "Next thing you know, we'll be passing Gangnam Style."

ANDY ZACH

"Don't be silly! That K-Pop song went over two billion hits! It would take twenty months like this one for us to get close. I'm sure this zombie turkey thing will die out within the month."

"But you know zombies—they get up again."

"Ha-ha. Look at me laugh. Seriously, I'm worried, Sam. Where's our next big story going to come from? We can't let the *Midley Beacon* be just a one-hit wonder! I've got twelve reporters busy all over Illinois—"

Sam's phone rang. "Turkey hotline," he answered. "I'm sorry to hear that, General Bagley... Uh-huh. Let me jot this down." Sam typed as General Bagley talked. "Thanks for calling and the tip, General Bagley."

"What's up?" Lisa asked.

"Thirteen turkey farms around the country have been infected. All of them have broken out of containment. We now have thirteen zombie turkey plagues in thirteen states, besides Illinois."

"Too bad it's not Friday the thirteenth! I just imagined our next headline: 'Thirteen Zombie Plagues on Friday!' Please list out the states, Sam."

"In alphabetic order: Buttery Turkeys, Connecticut; Caravel Turkeys, Virginia; Cottage Foods, Minnesota; Drevell Meats, Kansas; Freedom Turkeys, Iowa; House of Turkeys, Texas; Indian Turkey Farm, Indiana; Lazarus Turkey Farm, California; Omaha Turkeys, Nebraska; Parma Turkeys, Maryland; Speedy Turkeys, Ohio; The Best Turkeys, North Carolina; and Upper Peninsula Turkeys, Michigan."

"Whew! I'm glad I've hired those six new reporters! We can send one reporter to each state and turkey farm."

"I know I'm only an investigative reporter and not the editor, but that still leaves one not covered."

"Of course. We'll cover the one in California. Wouldn't you like to go to California? It'd be a like a second honeymoon!"

"A second honeymoon? We haven't even had a first! Working twelve to sixteen hours a day, cleaning up from turkey gore, driving all over the state—that was our honeymoon."

"Yes, and wasn't it romantic? Don't you want to do it all again?"

126

"I guess. If it's with you, that's good enough for me."

"You're so romantic! I'm 'good enough' for you! Your words will just go to my head! I'll swoon!" Lisa put her hand to her forehead and acted as if she were fainting. Sam jumped up and caught her.

"I guess you're romantic enough for me," she murmured, looking up at his face. They kissed. They were getting better at that.

Lisa called the twelve reporters and gave them their assignments. Lashon Bigelow got House of Turkeys, Texas.

She complained, "Oh, that won't work."

Lisa, surprised, asked, "Why not?"

"I'm still taking care of Rulon Miller while he's learning to use his prosthetic legs."

"Hmm. That leaves a hole in our reporting. How about covering Indian Turkey Farm? That's in Indiana, just a day trip from Chicago."

"I guess I can do that. But in traffic, that's a three-hour drive from Chicago!"

"You can use the corporate plane."

"We have a corporate plane?"

"I just bought one, a Piper Turbo Arrow, to get around Illinois faster."

"Did you buy a pilot too? I can't fly it!"

"I didn't buy a pilot, but I arranged to rent one. Dan Cosana. He's a retired pilot, he's a friend of mine, and loves to fly. His salary costs more than the plane."

"So how long will it take to get from Indian Turkey Farm to Chicago?"

"Using Midway, you can get to Chicago in an hour."

"OK. I'll give it a try. Lisa, you've got to know Rulon comes first in my life, ahead of work."

"So are you guys engaged or something?"

"Not yet, but I'm working on it!"

"You can always propose, like I did to Sam."

"You did that!? How did you do that?"

"After I decided I wanted to marry him, I asked him out on our first date. Then I proposed. I knew he would never ask me. We'd known each other since high school."

"When didja get married after that?"

"We got married by the justice of the peace the next day."

"When was that?"

"November 22nd, before Thanksgiving, when the zombie turkeys attacked Joliet."

"Pretty exciting. I may try that!"

"Leave out the getting attacked by zombie turkeys part. But first, fly to Indiana and get the story. I've found marriage to be a big distraction to work. I'm only getting about half the work done I used to get done."

"That's the kind of distraction I want!"

"It is kind of nice. Sam and I are going on a second honeymoon to California."

"Already?"

"We've got a zombie turkey breakout at a turkey farm to cover. I like reporting with Sam. That's my kind of honeymoon. In any event, I'll send Dan to pick you up and get you to Indian Turkey Farm tonight."

"You can just call him up anytime, and he'll go where you want?"

"Yep. The contract is for Illinois and any adjacent states. And I pay him plenty—trust me."

"OK, I'll get ready."

Chapter 13

Goodenow

Lashon called Rulon at his house and told him about her assignment.

"I've got another turkey call. I gotta report on the zombification of the Indian Turkey Farm in Indiana."

"I don't like this. I don't want you to be in danger."

"I've already been through the battle of Tinley Park and the battles at Chicago grocery stores. Anyway, these turkeys have flown the coop, as of today. I'm going to try to track them down, like Sam Melvin."

"If you need me, I'll come for you."

"Um, Rulon, you're missing two legs, and you aren't ready for prosthetics yet. And you're not a zombie turkey who can grow new legs."

"I get along fine in my wheelchair, fine enough to shoot a shotgun—or a flamethrower. My new turkey flamer arrived. It's specially designed for zombie turkeys! And I've got ten gallons of napalm. What kind of heat are you packing?"

"Lisa issued all her reporters flamethrowers and knives. Most of us also have other weapons. I don't want to mess around—I've got a chainsaw in my trunk."

"Is that what makes your trunk so attractive?"

"Tee-hee." Lashon giggled. For a big woman, she had a high-pitched laugh. Rulon said he loved it when she giggled. "I love it when you talk sexy. Well, honey, I'm at the airport. I gotta go. I love you."

"I love you too. Don't wait to call if you get in trouble."

"I won't. Bye."

"Bye."

Lashon met Dan in the civil aviation section of Midway. She saw a trim man of medium height, no taller than she, with light-gray hair. He looked ten years younger than the midsixties he was.

"Hi, you must be Lashon," he said.

"And you're Dan Cosana."

"Yep. I understand you're in a hurry?"

"Lisa is always in a hurry. I go where she sends me. So far, this job has been great. Let's get to Brimel, Indiana, where the Indian Turkey Farm is."

Inside the cockpit, after they had stowed her luggage, flamethrower, and chainsaw, Dan said, "I've planned the flight to take us to this local airstrip a couple miles from Brimel." Dan pointed on the map. "I've called the rental car company, and they'll pick you up there."

"Thanks! Are you doing travel agency services as well?"

"Not exactly. I needed a car myself, and I figured you wanted one."

"Very thoughtful of you! Thanks again."

"I really like not having to go through TSA inspections with a flamethrower, knives, and chainsaw," Lashon commented.

"Me too," Dan said.

They took off, with Lashon gripping her seat nervously. She had not flown in a single-engine prop plane before.

"Whee!" Lashon said. "I know this is just a prop job, but that was some take off."

"Yes, we've got a turbocharged engine and a hundred seventy horsepower. The retractable landing gear helps our speed too."

"How fast are we going?"

"A hundred and seventy knots. We'll be there in fifty minutes."

"That's not bad at all!"

* * *

Earlier that day, Sam and Lisa Melvin had left O'Hare airport for Reno, the closest airport to Lazarus Turkey Farm in California. They'd go from Reno, past Lake Tahoe, and into

California. Once there, they'd head for the Lazarus farm, outside of Hinton, about a half-hour drive.

After a smooth flight, they deplaned in Reno and picked up their rental car: a four-wheel drive SUV. They had specially shipped their weaponry to meet them at the airport, and loaded their car with it. They quickly drove to Hinton along I-80.

There they found the California National Guard in full battle with the 150,000 turkeys. The zombie turkeys had scattered into various flocks across the valley. In the valley floor, the turkeys really had nowhere to hide. Tanker planes used for forest fires bombed them with salt water. Then helicopters hit them with fléchettes. Soldiers with fléchette weapons would get the stragglers. These tactics had proven effective in Tinley Park a couple of days ago. One flock after another bit the dust.

Sam talked with one of the officers. "Say, can we go in and examine the remains of the turkey flock in that field?"

"Yes, our operations are done there."

Examining the remains of perhaps ten thousand turkeys in the field was like walking through mud with turkey salad spread on top. Sam and Lisa were prepared for the mess and put on their rubber boots before they left their car. The field, vegetation, and turkeys were all churned into an appalling slurry. After walking back and forth across the field, videotaping and narrating the success of the military, Lisa closed with, "And despite the name, Lazarus Turkey Farm, there will be no resurrection for these turkeys—they're salty turkey sausage."

"Nice turn of phrase."

"Thanks, Sam. There'll be something a little extra in your bed tonight."

"A bacon cheeseburger?"

"I didn't mean that, but that could be arranged."

"Let's go get it then."

"Let's go."

* * *

Lashon arrived at the Brimel airport with Dan. It really was in the middle of nowhere. She saw no control tower in the fading light, only a grass field. "How are we going to land in the dark?"

"Watch." Dan clicked the radio transmitter twice, then twice again. The landing lights came on. "A lot of fields are automatic and unmanned. They're activated by a radio signal from the plane at a certain frequency. They probably have someone here during the day."

"Cool!"

After a smooth landing, Dan said, "Here's my cell phone number. I'll be at the closest motel. Call me when you're ready to move."

"Thanks, Dan. I'll connect up with the local National Guard and police and find out what's going on. The news reports said they're 'pursuing the turkeys'—that means nothing. They probably don't have a clue."

"Maybe you'll be able to help them."

"Yeah, maybe. I know Sam could, and probably Lisa. They have a nose for turkeys. I'm more familiar with eating turkeys."

"Don't make them familiar with eating you!"

"Not while I have my flamethrower and chainsaw!" She patted them fondly. "Lisa got me these after the battle of Chicago and made me practice. They're a lot of fun. I actually like the chainsaw better, but the flamethrower is more effective."

"Do you got a gun?"

"Yep. A pump-action twelve gauge, loaded with 00 shot."

"You're ready then. Good luck!"

"Thanks. See you soon, I hope." Lashon carried her flamethrower and chainsaw toward the car Lisa had arranged for her to use. She found the key and loaded her weapons into the backseat.

Lashon's first call went to the local sheriff, Jeff Ridley. He agreed to an interview.

"I'm Lashon Bigelow, reporter with the *Midley Beacon*. Could you give me a summary of what steps you've taken since the Indian Turkey Farm was taken over by zombie turkeys?"

"Sure. I've read your paper online. We notified all the other turkey farms in Indiana—"

"Private ones too?"

"What do you mean?"

"In Illinois there were dozens of small, private turkey farms that sold organic turkeys online or to local organic food combines. These were not on record. They actually hid from public view. Over a hundred thousand zombie turkeys came from these farms."

"Whoa! We haven't investigated that. We'll do so tonight, as soon as I'm off the phone with you. Thanks for the tip!"

"That's a lesson learned in Illinois, Sheriff Ridley. We try to share what we learn with the public so all can defend against these zombies."

"Thanks again. After notifying the *public* turkey farms, we notified the local farms and towns. Every place is pretty much shut down now. We have a nine p.m. curfew, which is in two hours."

"What about your search efforts to find the turkeys?"

"We've used dogs and have found hundreds hibernating, which we dispatched."

"Not thousands?"

"No. We have not found the main flock yet."

"Where have you looked?"

"We've covered everything within five miles, and the rivers and woods up to ten miles away."

"Do you know what the army or Indiana National Guard is doing?"

"Yes, they're searching further out and scanning the forest with infrared scanners."

"They ought to know that won't work. When the zombie turkeys go into hibernation after eating, their body temperature drops, and they don't stand out on infrared. Who's your contact with the National Guard?"

"General Louise Hotchkiss."

"Could you give me her phone number?"

"Here's the official contact number. I don't have her cell number."

"Thanks. You've been a great help."

"You're welcome! Please visit Brimel when we aren't having a plague of zombies!"

"Thanks. Bye."

Lashon felt sure the turkey flock was somewhere in the deep woods, hibernating. That was how they hid near Joliet without being found. She looked at a map of the area.

There were plenty of places that would attract the turkeys: rivers, lakes, even golf courses and country clubs. But the fact the sheriff hadn't found them meant they were somewhere else. Brimel was near the Indiana/Illinois border. She looked over the border into Illinois.

"Hmmm, the Goodenow Nature Preserve. That's just the ticket. Seven miles away. They can get there in an hour, before dawn," she said to herself. She chuckled. "Even walking and running, they could make it in an hour."

Lashon called the Indiana National Guard. "Hi. This is Lashon Bigelow, reporter with the *Midley Beacon*. I'd like to talk about your search efforts for the zombie turkeys from the Indian Turkey Farm."

"Yes, ma'am. I'll connect you with Colonel Peterson."

"Colonel Peterson here," said a brisk voice in her ear.

"Hello, Colonel Peterson. This is Lashon Bigelow, reporter with the *Midley Beacon*. I'd like to talk about your search efforts for the zombie turkeys from the Indian Turkey Farm."

"We have covered all the areas within twenty miles of the farm, and we're working steadily outward."

"Have you searched within Illinois?"

"No, but we have notified General Bagley of the Illinois National Guard."

"Do you know what search operations they are conducting?"

"No, ma'am, although I believe they've moved forces along the border."

"Thank you, Colonel. Good-bye."

Lashon then called General Bagley. Although she hadn't talked with him, Lisa had given her his number. The worst he could do was hang up on her.

"General Bagley," said a gruff voice.

"This is Lashon Bigelow, reporter with the *Midley Beacon*. I'd like to talk about your search efforts for the zombie turkeys from the Indian Turkey Farm."

"*Midley Beacon*? You've done good work there. Did you get my number from Lisa?"

"Yes."

"Please don't give it out to anyone else. This is my personal cell. In the future, please work through our official public number."

"OK. Would you be able to answer any questions about your operations in Illinois?"

"Briefly, yes. We have cordoned the Indiana/Illinois border. No turkey incursions have been reported."

"When did the cordon get established?"

"By eight a.m. the morning, after the break out from the Indian Turkey Farm."

"Have you conducted any search operations further inside the border?"

"No, ma'am. We do not believe the turkeys could have completely broken out of the farm and come over the border by the morning afterward."

"Thank you, General." No sense in pointing out the turkeys had escaped his cordons twice before. Hanging up, she immediately dialed Dan Cosana. "Hi, Dan. I'm going to drive over the border to Illinois to search for some turkeys. I'll be at the Goodenow Nature Preserve. I'll leave it up to you if you want to move the plane or not. I don't mind driving back here."

"How far is that?"

"About seven miles from Brimel."

"If you don't mind, I'll just stay here. I'm about three miles outside of Brimel, just a couple of miles from the airport."

"That's fine. See you later, probably tomorrow."

Lashon checked her gear. This was one of the best times to look for turkeys, just after sunset or just before dawn. She'd look until ten p.m., go back to the motel, and then get up early the next morning.

The drive to the nature preserve went quickly. She first drove completely around and through the nature preserve, very slowly, looking for any movement. She saw some deer, but no turkeys. She parked at the nature center and mounted her flamethrower on her back. No sense in taking chances. She walked along the scout path heading toward Plum Creek. Zombie turkeys usually followed waterways. She listened carefully, although why, she didn't know. Turkeys were quieter than deer in the woods, when they weren't attacking lone pedestrians, like her.

She left the scout path and followed the creek path. She saw some blotches of white along the creek. Turkeys. Domestic turkeys, probably zombie, resting or hibernating. Her throat tightened, as well as her gut. She really wasn't too smart in doing this alone—but neither had Sam been. She backed off as quietly as she could and crept along the path back to her car.

With the lights of the parking lot peeking through the trees, she relaxed. Whew! She made it. This'd be a big coup for her and—

"Gobble! Gobble!" Dozens of turkeys attacked her, from the front and from the back. "Ow!" she yelled. Those bastards *hurt*.

"Eat flame, suckers!" She turned around with a practiced pivot. She had the delight of seeing several covered in napalm and the rest run.

"Gobble! Gobble! Gobble! Gobble! Gobble! Gobble! Gobble! Gobble!"

"Feet, don't fail me now!" she said to herself as she ran down the path. With adrenaline running through her, the thirty-pound flamethrower tank didn't feel that heavy, but it did bang uncomfortably. A sudden memory flashed of running laps in her high school basketball team practices. She hadn't thought of that for years.

A solid phalanx of zombie turkeys blocked the path in front of her, just before the parking lot.

"Come back for more? Eat fire and die!" She sprayed napalm ferociously. It didn't ignite. The spark ignition failed. Without thinking, she leapt toward the nearest tree, shedding the useless tank with a shrug of her shoulders. In case she needed any additional motivation, the turkeys pecked her butt all the way up.

The turkeys did not give up trying to reach her in the tree. They flew up and attacked her. She wielded her bowie knife, Rulon's gift to her. He'd had it inscribed *To Lashon, from Rulon*. After about ten minutes of fighting them off, her arm was getting tired. She switched to her left arm. She wasn't particularly dexterous with her left, but she didn't have to be. Twenty-pound turkeys who flew straight at you didn't require much precision to strike. The most disheartening thing was, she'd stab one through the heart, it'd drop fifteen feet to the ground with a satisfying *thud*, and then it'd stagger to its feet five minutes later and fly back up fifteen minutes later.

She sat astride a tree limb, sitting on her sore and bleeding butt, fighting off crazed turkeys, shivering in the cold and damp. She had no hope of relief until the morning. She didn't think she could make it. Maybe Rulon could if he were in her place; he was tough as nails and had the endurance of a horse. They had gone jogging together, he in his wheelchair and she afoot. She had started out slow, thinking to do him a favor, but he had gone longer and faster than she could.

Holding the knife in her left hand, she called on her phone with her right. "Sheriff Ridley? Sorry to bug you, but I'm up a tree. Literally. I'm being attacked by zombie turkeys."

"How many, Ms. Bigelow?"

"How many? Oh, a couple hundred around the tree, plus however many thousand escaped from the Indian Turkey Farm in total."

"Where are you?"

"The Goodenow Nature Preserve, in Illinois. I'm on the scout path, within sight of the parking lot. My car is the only one there."

"I'll send a car right away. I'll also call the sheriff over there in Illinois."

"Thanks. Try to hurry. I'm getting tired of fending them off with my knife."

"We're leaving now."

Lashon felt better—not as good as in her hotel room, but she had some hope.

The sheriff was as good as his word; the car pulled up in about ten minutes. Thousands of turkeys surrounded it. She heard the *boom! boom!* of the automatic shotgun, and then another. Several turkeys exploded into blood and feathers; the rest continued their onslaught undeterred. The ones attacking her did not stop; she had to switch to her right hand again.

Another sheriff's car pulled up. More shotgun fire. Some pistol and rifle fire. She thought wearily how the past week had taught her to distinguish guns from one another by sound. Still, thousands of zombie turkeys flocked around the two cars. Eventually, the deputies ran out of ammo and drove away.

Lashon's hope collapsed. Her right arm was fatigued, and she switched to the left again. The zombie turkeys had given her some nasty pokes on both her arms, and she bled from them. "Good thing it's not contagious to humans. I need to get a break from these zombies." She climbed another fifteen feet up the tree.

The turkeys still attacked her, but far less frequently. Unfortunately, the weather was getting colder. *Good thing we're not having a blizzard,* she thought.

In desperation she called General Bagley.

"Lashon, I told you not to call me at this number! Go through normal channels!" he yelled.

"I found the zombie turkeys in Illinois," she said wearily.

"Where?" he barked.

"In Goodenow Nature Preserve. They have me up a tree, and I'm getting tired of fighting them off and holding on."

"All right," he said, mollified. "We'll send troops over there right away."

While she waited for the army, she gave Rulon a call.

"Hi, Lashon. How are things going?"

"Crappy. I'm surrounded by zombie turkeys, thirty feet up a tree. I'm bleeding and cold and thirsty."

"Crap! Where are you?"

"Goodenow Nature Preserve."

"I'll be right there."

"Wait! No! You're two legs short!"

"No problem. I'll manage. Bye. I gotta use the phone to call the door-to-door bus."

"What?! A door-to-door bus? Rulon! Rulon! You lunatic redneck!"

Rulon called the door-to-door service for disabled people. He'd started using them ever since he lost his feet. He planned to hijack the bus and drive it to Goodenow Nature Preserve. He knew how to get there; he had hunted turkeys near there. Now he would hunt turkeys in the park.

"Hello. This is the Chicago Door-to-Door Service."

"Hi. I need to get to Goodenow Nature Preserve right away."

"That is outside our service area."

"How about Calumet City or Thornton?" Once there, he'd take over the bus.

"We can take you to either of those places."

"How soon can you pick me up?"

"We need at least one hour's notice."

"What!? My girlfriend's life depends upon this."

"I'm sorry. You should call the police or 911."

"Forget about it!" He hung up. Now he had to go to plan B. He had thought of this plan when Lashon first told him she would investigate the Indian Turkey Farm. He thought hijacking the door-to-door bus was less risky, so he tried that first. He had no idea they were so slow.

He had already packed his pickup truck with his flamethrower and shotguns. A new load of one thousand rounds of 00 shot had just come in, and he had it wedged in there, next to the barrel of napalm. He grabbed some warm blankets and a first-aid kit for Lashon—she'd probably need them—and wheeled his chair down the impromptu ramp he had made of three-quarter-inch sheets of plywood. The ramp sloped too steeply for regulation, but he didn't care; it worked.

Rulon had puzzled over how to drive his car, missing his right foot at the ankle and his left leg at the knee. He could move the seat up and push with his right leg stump, but the stump was pretty tender. It'd be a bitch to drive the hour to Goodenow pushing it on the accelerator, let alone the brake. He'd do it if he had to, but he had come up with a better idea.

After collapsing his wheelchair and lugging it into the passenger's side, he closed the door and pulled out his crutch from the backseat. He would use that to work the accelerator and brake. He'd been practicing this technique in his driveway, but this was his first time on the streets. "You only live once," he told himself. And he intended to speed too.

He took I-90 to I-94 to IL-394, and he never went below seventy miles per hour. He averaged ninety. Still, crazier drivers passed him several times. Chicago drivers! He was glad it wasn't snowing. Not that he would have slowed; it just would have made driving riskier.

Rulon made the forty-mile trip in half an hour. He pulled into the parking lot and saw the closely packed flock of turkeys. He bashed his way through them and pulled next to Lashon's car and called her on the cell phone.

"You idiot!" she answered.

"Hey, baby, I've come to save the day. Where are you?"

"About thirty feet up a tree, just down the scout path, near the parking lot. Don't you dare leave your car! The military are already here. I've heard their gunships north of here."

"I've got it under control! I'll see you soon. Bye!" He grabbed his flamethrower, stuck it out the window, and started flaming turkeys. After clearing the parking lot, he put his truck in four-wheel drive and steered down the scout path. He didn't see Lashon, but he saw turkeys crowded around a tree. He flamed them, and they fled.

His phone rang.

"You *idiot*! You've set the tree on fire!"

"Oops! Sorry about that. Lemme get my fire extinguisher."

"You have a fire extinguisher?"

"Yup. I had one for my truck before I got a flamethrower. You never want any fire in your pickup. Here we go." He sprayed the burning trunk of the tree. It took the whole extinguisher to put out the napalm, but he did it.

"Come to papa, baby!" Rulon called up into the tree.

"Don't look at me."

"Why? I want to look!"

"Because my butt is hanging out!"

"All the more reason to look!"

"Rulon Miller, I swear I'll cut off more than your legs with this bowie knife you gave me!"

"It'll be worth it, for one glimpse of your fair buttocks."

"My buttocks are anything but fair." She laughed as she reached the ground.

"I can see that. But all buttocks look black at night."

Lashon burst into helpless laughter. "Move over, big and ugly," she said as she opened the driver's-side door. "Oh, so that's how you got here. You used your crutch to drive. Pretty clever, but really dangerous."

"Baby, I live for danger. That's why I love you."

"I love you too, but I don't know why."

"It's my full beard!"

"No, that's your worst feature."

"Trust me—I look worse without it."

"I don't think that's possible."

"Oh, you wound me!"

"Listen to us, bickering like an old married couple. Why don't you propose to me?"

"OK. Lashon Bigelow, will you marry me?"

"You bet."

* * *

While the Melvins were plodding through turkey mud in California, and Lashon was up a tree in Goodenow, Serena Fields traveled to Caravel Turkeys, fifteen miles west of Norfolk, Virginia. The flock of sixty thousand zombie turkeys flew directly into the crowded city of Norfolk. Fortunately, plenty of military and ex-military personnel had their military-issued arms as well as extras they purchased. They didn't have as many flamethrowers as in Chicago and the rest of Illinois, but they had plenty of military service knives—and lots of salt water.

By this time, everyone in the US knew the routine with zombie turkeys: shoot or stun them, and cut them in half. Spray them with salt water, if you had it. A flock that surged to the shore was stopped cold by the salt spray off the Norfolk docks. The citizens then slaughtered the dazed turkeys and put them in their freezers for Christmas.

One desperate person, under siege by hundreds of turkeys, opened his garage to the zombie flock, calling them using Rulon Miller's All Turkey Call, purchased from the *Midley Beacon* website. He opened a can of propane and closed the garage door as he slipped out the back. With the garage full of turkeys and propane gas, he threw a Molotov cocktail through the window, blowing up the garage and the turkeys with a fuel air explosion.

The same day, Bret Brown visited Cottage Foods Turkey Farm in Lafayette, Minnesota. The farmer, Elmer McDonald, was spraying most of his flock with salt water daily. An eTurkey delivery of zombie turkeys contaminated one barn of about ten thousand turkeys after the daily spraying. They were all contained in the building. McDonald turned off the heat, turned on his fire sprinkling system, and froze them all overnight, thanks to Minnesota's subzero weather. McDonald managed to sell the turkeys on the internet as whole, frozen, zombie turkeys. He got the idea from the *Midley Beacon* website selling the zombie turkey sausage. The episode opened his eyes to the internet as a sales channel; he had never sold through the internet before. Desperate times called for desperate measures.

Meanwhile, reporter Sarah Phillips investigated Drevell Meats in near Manhattan, Kansas. The zombie turkey plague seemed far away to the managers of this farm, and they had not prepared for the plague. This factory farm had over 150,000 turkeys, and they all zombified.

The owner called the Kansas National Guard, who arrived with AH-64 helicopters armed with fléchettes. They followed the standard anti-zombie techniques developed in Illinois: bomb the flocks with salt water from tankers and hit them with fléchettes from the air and ground. On the wide plains of Kansas, the turkeys had nowhere to hide. Also, there were fewer wild turkeys to add to their ranks. The National Guard completely wiped out the zombie turkeys. Citizens who were unarmed simply went into their tornado shelters. Even at the Drevell Meats farm, the workers had hidden in the shelters in the buildings and stayed safe while the zombie turkeys escaped, to their death. Amazingly, no one had been killed in Kansas.

That evening, Rob Peterson reported on Freedom Turkeys in Bingingham, Iowa. An eTurkey delivery of over a thousand turkeys contaminated the farm. The receiving manager, Eldon Cruikshank, quarantined the eTurkeys in a separate building. Sadly, the contagion managed to spread through the air to the nearest barn of about five thousand turkeys. The workers kept the turkeys confined to these two barns while they burned them down using flamethrowers.

At the same time, Roger Smith, one of Lisa's newly hired reporters, went to House of Turkeys in Lubbock, Texas. Like the Kansas turkey farm, they were unprepared, and eighty thousand turkeys caught the disease. Cleverly, the local fire department used a tanker truck and hundreds of bags of salt to make the farm's own water pond saline, and then firefighters pumped and sprayed the salt water on the zombie turkey flock. Not only did this stop the plague, but the farm recovered most of the eighty thousand turkeys.

Tina Piscara, another new reporter, went to Omaha Turkeys, in Omaha, Nebraska. They also used salt spray on their turkeys, which prevented the eTurkey zombies from contaminating them. However, five hundred eTurkeys became zombies in the receiving dock, killing some of the personnel there. They then flew into the wide-open spaces of Nebraska. Using dogs, the National Guard tracked the flock down to the roosting site near the Platte River, where the troops dispatched them with their shoulder-mounted rocket launchers.

Newly-hired Maryann Ogilvy reported on Parma Turkeys, in Cumberland, Maryland. They too had a quarantine on the eTurkey shipment of seven hundred turkeys. They turned zombie while in quarantine and escaped through the wire mesh of the barn, contaminating another ten thousand turkeys, who also escaped. The flock of almost eleven thousand attacked Cumberland. Most civilians stayed indoors and shot from their windows. The military got most of the birds with salt water bombing. However, Maryland had a lot of wild turkeys, and thousands transformed into zombies. The Maryland Department of Transportation snowplowed some, and farmers harrowed more, and the military tracked down still more, but state officials believed at least a thousand wild zombie turkeys remained in the woods and streams of Maryland. In an emergency session, the legislature passed a law for a perpetual open season on zombie turkeys. (Thousands of turkey hunters descended on Maryland from all over the country. Before spring came, they had wiped out the zombie turkeys. The revenue from the visiting hunters more than paid for the damage caused by the zombies. This gave Maryland Natural Resources and Tourism departments the idea of infecting a flock of zombie turkeys each winter, during the slow tourist season, and opening hunting for them.)

Another new reporter, Preston Lafarge, reported from Speedy Turkeys farm in Centerville, Ohio. This was a massive turkey farm of 125,000 turkeys. The managers had secure barns, and they sprayed the eTurkey turkeys with salt water when they arrived. Nonetheless, the bacteria somehow got into three of their barns, and thirty thousand turkeys zombified. Again, the winter weather helped as workers sprayed these turkeys with plain water and froze them in unheated barns.

Preston pointed out the success of selling frozen zombie turkeys over the internet, and the Speedy Turkeys farm speedily did so. The competition to sell frozen zombie turkeys drove the price down to three dollars per pound. (This became standard practice for turkey farms around the country each winter. After the big turkey season of Thanksgiving, Christmas, and New Year's, they would infect some of their flock with the zombie turkey plague and then freeze and sell these turkeys.)

Charlie Gomez arrived in Hartford, Connecticut, that afternoon, and drove the forty miles to Buttery Turkeys, where eTurkey had delivered its plague-ridden turkeys—one of many farms ordering from this gigantic, nationwide turkey-producing firm. Fortunately, "only" fifty thousand turkeys had turned, and "only" twenty thousand escaped. An enterprising employee had used a spare can of gas from his car to set fire to one of the two barns, and he'd killed thirty thousand zombie turkeys in the conflagration. However, three farmworkers were killed. Charlie connected their newly widowed wives with the ZoTWHA, which was growing faster than a zombie turkey could grow a leg.

Charlie discovered the remaining turkeys had attacked a nearby farm. A Tuffield turkey trap, bought on the internet from the *Midley Beacon* website, killed hundreds in its wood chipper before the zombie flock moved on to easier pastures. Charlie interviewed the happy farm couple, who gave personal testimonies about the trap's effectiveness. Charlie posted the interview on the *Midley Beacon* website.

This was a double human-interest story: first, an embattled farmer defeated the terrible zombie turkeys, and second, the poor widow of a man killed by zombie turkeys made a killing in zombie turkey traps. Charlie smiled to himself. Puns were good. And the more Tuffield turkey traps that sold from the *Midley* website, the more the *Midley Beacon* and all the reporters profited.

The zombie turkeys hit the town of Liberty next, where civilians defended their homes with flamethrowers, Molotov cocktails, and shotguns. By this time, the flock had diminished to ten thousand. After the citizens of Liberty halved the number of turkeys, the National Guard, search dogs, and local militia dispatched the rest. Charlie wrote up his final story, posted it, and headed home.

Gail Cunningham witnessed the battle at The Best Turkeys farm, ten miles outside Raleigh, North Carolina. Again, the farm did not expect or prepare for the zombie plague. The eTurkeys arrived, and 180,000 turkeys were infected and escaped, killing most of the farmworkers. Hitting Raleigh, they went through the town, deterred only by Molotov cocktails and flamethrowers owned by the local citizens. The National Guard encircled Raleigh and went block to block, wiping them out. The local Caterpillar dealer also helped with salt water–filled tanker trucks. The zombies killed over two thousand people before the last turkeys were carved, roasted, or salted down.

Finally, George Underhill went to Upper Peninsula Turkeys outside Ironton, Michigan. In the depth of a normal winter, when the eTurkey truck arrived with zombie turkeys, the farm employees grabbed a fire hose and sprayed them, quickly freezing them. The pneumatic contagion, however, still contaminated one of their barns. Before the turkeys escaped, the employees bravely walked among the cages, spraying them with salt water. This saved their turkeys, to be made into turkey bacon, later that month.

Chapter 14

Schaumburg

Dr. Galloway was troubled. He'd been experimenting with ECG (E. coli Gallopavo), the newly discovered zombie turkey bacteria, to see if it could transfer to any other species. He'd tried injecting it and feeding it to various species, under various circumstances. It didn't seem to transfer.

However, when he experimented with the GMO corn that had caused the ECG and fed it to different birds and animals and then checked the fecal matter for modified E. coli, many animals had produced a zombie mutation of their specific E. coli. When he tested the modified E. coli for each species, some animals metamorphosed into zombies. He didn't worry about the vegetarians; zombie deer, cows, pigeons, and bunny rabbits didn't seem as dangerous as omnivorous birds like turkeys—or chickens. Yes, chickens could become zombies if they got the bacteria intravenously or aspirated it. That was a real problem, because while there were millions of turkeys, there were billions of chicken in the US.

He had contacted Corn-All about his connection between ECG and their GMO corn. They admitted they had modified the corn as he had suspected, but it had been an overall failure in preventing disease—it prevented ear rot, but other diseases were not stopped. They assured him they were not making any more of the corn and that the Bartonville farmer's field had been their sole test field.

That had reassured him, but when he found out about the possible cross-species contaminations from the corn, he called Corn-All again. Specifically, he asked where all the modified corn had gone. They said they had disposed of it all after testing it. They didn't want anyone else to reverse engineer their corn, as Dr. Galloway had done.

Dr. Galloway felt better then. His lab had identified some effective antibiotics for the bacteria. He licensed the formula to various veterinary medicine companies. The companies put the medicines into mass production, with generous federal subsidies to accelerate their development of anti-zombie antibiotics. He'd be financially secure for the rest of his life on this work. His zombie turkey work, even more than his turkey cloning efforts, had made him the chief expert on turkeys in the world.

He put the finishing touches on his paper on the bacteria and submitted the final copy to the *Journal of Turkey Medicine*. He hoped he'd get some recognition for his work. Money was nice, but academic recognition was even more important to him.

* * *

Sam and Lisa documented the death of the turkeys at the Lazarus Turkey Farm and uploaded their stories. Lashon told the story about Indian Turkey Farm from Indiana, complete with her detective work finding the turkeys in Goodenow Nature Reserve, and being surrounded in a tree, and heroically being rescued by Rulon.

Lisa loved the human-interest angle—a handicapped man rescued a damsel in distress, although Lashon, at nearly six feet tall and close to two hundred pounds, didn't quite fit the "damsel" motif. The fact he proposed to her added more spice to the story, and the readers ate it up.

Charlie had reported on Buttery Turkeys from Connecticut, and the other reporters had filled in from the zombie turkey breakouts across the country. In each of the thirteen states, the outbreaks had been contained, controlled, and eliminated. The whole country breathed a sigh of relief as it prepared for Christmas.

Lisa called Dr. Galloway when they returned to Chicago from California on the Monday after Thanksgiving. Sam listened to her side of the conversion at the airport.

"Hello, Dr. Galloway. Have you learned anything new about the turkey disease?... You have?... Could we stop by and interview you? We've just arrived in Chicago... Great. We'll see you at two.

"We've got another interview with Dr. Galloway. I want to find out more about this zombie turkey disease, and he said he's got more on it," she told Sam.

After eating at the airport, they left for the Turkey Institute, where they met Dr. Galloway.

"Hello, Mr. and Mrs. Melvin."

"You can call us Lisa and Sam, Doctor," Lisa said.

He smiled. "In that case, you can call me Ed. I'm only a lab rat in my ivory tower, while you are world-famous reporters."

Sam laughed. "I don't feel famous!"

"You are, to me at least. I read the *Midley Beacon* website every day. What can I do for you?"

"You mentioned you were going to follow up with Corn-All about their GMO corn that caused zombiism. Whatever happened to the corn from that field?" Lisa asked.

"I called Corn-All about that corn. They said they were dissatisfied with the disease-prevention results and destroyed the corn. Er, make that 'disposed of the corn.'"

"How did they dispose of it?" Lisa asked.

"I didn't pursue that. I trust my contact there, and I'm sure he's telling me the truth."

"Who is your contact? We'd like to talk to him or her," Lisa said.

"I don't think he would mind. Dr. Ken Wu. We were classmates together at Illinois State."

"Thanks, Ed. Is that all you've found out since your last news conference?" Lisa asked.

Dr. Galloway hesitated. "There is one other thing. We did extensive tests to see if we could transfer the bacteria to other animals."

"Whoa! That would be bad, really bad," Sam interjected.

"Yes. We confirmed the ECG bacterium cannot infect any other animal. However, when we fed the GMO corn to various animals, some of them produced mutated E. coli bacteria that could then infect members of that species with zombiism."

"What other animals were susceptible?" Lisa asked.

"Well, chickens are my main worry."

"Wow," Sam said. "If they go zombie, I don't know if we have enough bullets to kill them all!"

"This is huge," Lisa said. "We've got to find out where that corn went. 'Disposed'—but how?"

"You said 'main worry,'" Sam continued. "What else went zombie?"

"Well, squirrels and rabbits and cows too, but they are vegetarian."

"Are those all?" Lisa asked.

"Those are all we tested. Remember, our focus is poultry, not other species. We just tried those because they're common wildlife and domestic animals that might eat corn."

"So there could be other animals that could go zombie from this corn?" Lisa continued.

"Theoretically, yes."

"Oh, baby," sighed Sam.

"Do you have any other findings?" Lisa asked.

"Not on ECG or zombiism. Do you have enough for your story?"

"Yes, but before we publish, we're going to talk with Dr. Wu of Corn-All."

"I'll call him and tell him you're coming."

"Thank you. Good-bye."

Dr Wu worked at the Corn-All headquarters in Schaumburg, a suburb of Chicago. He agreed to talk with them that very afternoon. He met them at the entrance of the building. He was a slim man with black hair and glasses.

"Hello. I'm Dr. Wu. You must be Sam and Lisa Melvin."

"Hello, Dr. Wu. Thank you for agreeing to meet with us on such short notice and answer some questions about your company's GMO corn," Lisa said.

"Let's go to my office." Once there, he said, "Now what would you like to know?"

"This is regarding the GMO corn that was grown near Bartonville, that Dr. Galloway identified as transferring part of its DNA to wild turkeys' E. coli," Lisa began.

"Yes. He discussed that with me. I cannot say whether that particular strain of corn actually caused that bacterial mutation or not."

"That's not really necessary. Dr. Galloway will publish a paper on the subject. What we'd like to know is, where did that corn go?"

"Ah. We have a standard disposal process for all our GMO corn that does not meet our exacting standards. This experimental corn failed to achieve its goal, and we disposed of it."

"How did you dispose of it?"

"We hire a trucking company to dump it in a landfill."

"That seems pretty safe," Sam commented. "Which company is it?"

"Illinois Waste Company."

"Do you have a contact there?" Lisa asked.

"I'm not in charge of buying their services. As far as I know, they've been our disposal service for years. I really can't tell you any more about them."

"OK. That was all we really wanted to know. Thank you for your time. Good-bye."

As soon as she hopped into their car in the parking lot, Lisa called Illinois Waste Company.

"Hello, this is Lisa Melvin of the *Midley Beacon*. We'd like to do an article about your company. Who can I talk with there?"

"I'll connect you with our public relations manager, Mindy Hawthorne."

"Mindy Hawthorne, how can I help you?" a cheery voice said.

"Hello, this is Lisa Melvin of the *Midley Beacon*. We'd like to do an article about your company. When can we meet to talk and take a tour of your facilities?"

"Thank you for your interest!" Mindy said brightly. "We'll be closing for the day soon, but I'll be happy to talk with you at nine a.m. tomorrow morning and show you our facilities."

"Great," Lisa said. "Could we make a video of your facility?"

"Sure thing!"

"See you at nine a.m.! Bye." Lisa turned to Sam. "It's on! We're going to get to the bottom of this!"

The next morning Sam and Lisa arrived at Illinois Waste Company and met Mindy Hawthorne in the company's lobby.

Mindy was an attractive, well-dressed woman with a warm smile and reddish-brown hair that framed her face.

"Hi. I'm Lisa Melvin, and this is my coworker and husband, Sam Melvin. We'd like to understand how your operation works."

"Sure. Waste disposal is a fascinating business. Our distinct competency is in providing long-term, low-cost disposal services to companies the way they want, when they want, at the price they want."

"Let's start at the beginning. Say you have a long-term contract, and the company contacts you to dispose of something. What happens next?"

"We send a truck to the agreed-upon location and pick it up within a day."

"What if it takes more than one truck load?"

"We send as many trucks as are necessary."

"Do you bill by truck or by weight?"

"Neither. We have an agreed-upon contract for a year with an estimated number of truckloads. If it goes over or under that estimate for the month, we make an adjustment for that month."

"Sounds good. Where do you dispose of the waste?"

"It depends upon the material. Clean fill goes into landfills."

"So would grain be considered clean fill?"

"Yes, of course."

"And what about toxic materials, like paints or gasoline or napalm?"

"We have a contracted partner for that material. Our partner will take it and safely extract any useful material and dispose of the rest according to regulation."

"And what about biohazardous material, like needles and hospital waste?"

"That kind of material is incinerated on site."

"Could we take a tour of your site?"

"Sure." They saw the incinerator, the recycling bins, and the landfill.

"So this is where grain would be disposed?" Lisa continued her questioning.

"Yes, and other clean fill: rocks, gravel, and dirt."

"Could we talk with one of your truck drivers?"

"Sure." They walked over to a truck driver dumping a load of dirt. When he finished, he jumped out of his truck and walked up to them.

Mindy introduced them. "This is Mark Victor. Mark, this is Lisa and Sam Melvin from the *Midley Beacon*. They're doing a story on our operation. They'd like to talk with you."

"OK."

"Mark, have you ever hauled grain from Corn-All?"

"Yeah, I got that job a couple times. I think every driver has done that run."

"And do you always dump the grain here, not anyplace else?"

"Yeah."

"And how long is the grain exposed before it is covered up? Do you ever see birds or animals feeding on it?"

"I guess it's exposed until the next load comes in. I never seen any animals or birds on it."

"How many loads come in here a day?"

"Fifty or so."

"That's over eight hours? Six or seven an hour?"

"We run twelve hours a day," Mindy commented. "There are two eight-hour shifts that overlap for four hours during the busy part of the day."

"How many drivers are there?"

"Eight. Two shifts of four each."

"That's all very helpful. Thank you!"

As they drove away, Sam commented, "That seemed pretty boring to me. Are we really going to make a story of this?"

"It's all how it's framed, Sam. The key things we learned are that there are, on average, four to five loads dropped an hour. That's ten to fifteen minutes per load. That's not much exposure for the grain to cause animals to go zombie. However, if it's the last load at night, then it's exposed for twelve hours or more before it's covered up. That's the main exposure."

"That doesn't seem like much exposure to me. I don't see many animals around here, and the nearest woods are miles away."

"All true. Let's maintain a watch on this landfill overnight and see if there are any animals at night."

"OK. That does sound boring though."

"Boring can be good. We can spend the night kissing and making out."

"What can we see at night anyway?"

"Everything—with these." Lisa showed him her new night-vision goggles. "I got them to help see zombie turkeys at night. Every reporter got a pair. Lashon could have used them tracking down the Indian Turkey Farm turkeys—or you could have used them around Hanna City. Let's see what we can see. We'll come back here after dinner."

The night passed uneventfully, except for their torrid make-out sessions. They used the night-vision goggles and saw a deer or two on the property and something that looked like a raccoon or possum, but nothing else.

The next morning, after a nap at the hotel, Lisa said, "You wanted to know how the story would be interesting. We now have proof that the GMO grain has been disposed of and further zombification of other animals is unlikely. We'll combine this with our report on Dr. Galloway's findings that other animals can go zombie, but only from that grain."

"That does sound interesting. You always see the big picture, Lisa."

"And you always dig out the necessary details, Sam."

"We make a good team."

"You can say that again, but that would be cliché. Come up with something fresh, novel, interesting, with a human-interest side."

"How about 'we go together like a horse and carriage'?"

"Trite—from a song. Try again."

"We go together like 'GMO corn and zombie turkeys'?"

"Not bad—original, interesting, but maybe not a human-interest side."

"I'm not writing for the paper—I'm talking to you!"

"In that case," Lisa said with a smile, "it's 'good enough' for me—like you!"

Lisa and Sam came back to the *Midley Beacon* office after two weeks away, three weeks before Christmas. As Lisa had feared, as the turkey zombie crisis wound down, their page hits fell. Zombie turkey fear still gripped the nation: the zombie turkey traps, flamethrowers, shotgun manufacturers, and, surprisingly, T-Shirts still sold like coffee at a writers' convention.

Lisa also had added a line of hoodies, coasters, and coffee cups. They flew out of inventory like zombie turkeys out of hell. But nothing beat the zombie turkey sausage.

***

The high sales volume of the sausage delighted Betty Tuffield. Although billed as "not fit for human consumption," an internet fad had emerged, with people cooking it and eating it and posting videos of their meals on Vine or YouTube. Betty had long ago run out of sausage from her farm, but the second battle of Tom's turkey farm had netted over a thousand turkey carcasses suitable for sausages.

Also, selling hundreds of Tuffield turkey traps had given her a steady supply of ground turkey from around the country. She paid other zombie turkey widows and other turkey farms to have it shipped to her enterprise, where her workers packed sausages in the empty turkey barn and then shipped them around the world. She also raised the price of the sausage to fifteen dollars a pound. Since Tuffield Genuine Zombie Turkey Sausage was the original, she could sell it at a premium.

She also kept a flock of zombie turkeys in steel cages on her farm. This way she'd always have some to add to the sausage. She made more money than Tom ever had with their organic turkeys. This gave her solace for his death.

And Hank Williams also was a great comfort. He often visited her with his family, and she visited his turkey farm. It was operational again, but seeing and smelling the turkeys gave her a pang of sad nostalgia, sweetened by their growing friendship. Perhaps their friendship would become something more.

* * *

Lisa created a *Remember the Zombie Widow* blog in the paper to keep that Tuffield-Williams human-interest story alive. Mrs. Helen Yoder said she enjoyed writing about the latest news from the ZoTWHA. The advertising from the blog supplemented her income. Amos's insurance had paid off their debts and given her a good nest egg to start a new life.

The late-night comedians milked the crisis for all the jokes they could find. A series of "Why did the zombie turkey cross the road?" jokes proliferated and, thankfully, died, never to be resurrected.

But the zombie turkey threat ended with the military wiping out the thirteen turkey farms infected from eTurkey.

eTurkey, not surprisingly, had gone out of business due to the liability lawsuits for sending infected turkeys to farms around the country. The corporation lacked the funds necessary to defend the many lawsuits it faced. Its main rival, eGobble, quickly gobbled up their market share. eGobble advertised that it tested every turkey for zombie bacteria by tests from the Turkey Institute before shipping. A salt spray every hour protected the turkeys in transit from infection.

Corn-All had suffered some bad public relations but managed to fend off liability lawsuits, and gained public goodwill by setting up a fund to help the victims of the zombie turkeys. They also contributed to the ZoTWHA (led by Mrs. Tuffield and Mrs. Yoder). They paid for a pop-up ad on the ZoTWHA website. They also started a line of non-GMO seed corn and other non-GMO corn products.

Lisa moved into Sam's house when they got back to Midley. Her house was much nicer, so she rented that out. Sam's house gave her great scope for redecorating.

Bored with the inactivity in the office, Lisa turned to Sam and said, "What will you wear to Lashon and Rulon's wedding on Christmas Eve?"

"Not much choice. I have one suit. I'll wear that."

"We *do* have enough money to buy you a new suit—or two or three!"

"It's in perfectly good shape, and I only wear it once a year, at most."

"Fine—be boring!"

"You married a boring man."

"Did you hear what Lashon is wearing?"

"White, I assume."

"Yes, but she's going to have a fine red ribbon spiraling down from her veil to her train to get a candy cane–striped effect."

"Creative. What will the bridesmaids wear?"

"Red dresses with a white ribbon. The theme will be red and white."

"Sounds good. Where will they marry?"

"At Lashon's home church in Gary. Didn't you read the wedding invitation?"

"No. It's on the refrigerator. I'll look at the directions the day before we go."

"You're such a...man!"

"And aren't you glad?"

"Yes."

* * *

Sam and Lisa were scheduled to appear on the Oprah Winfrey show the week before Christmas. Oprah greeted them ebulliently, in her usual fashion. "And tonight we have the two key reporters who made a name for themselves on the internet reporting on the zombie turkey crisis at the risk of their lives, and then got married in the middle of it, Sam and Lisa Melvin!"

After hugging each of them, Oprah pointed to their chairs and said, "Let's begin at the beginning. Sam, you were the first one who broke the story on the zombie turkeys. Tell us how it began."

And so Oprah led them to tell the whole story of their adventures together. At one point she asked Sam, "When did you realize Lisa was interested in you romantically?"

"Not until she proposed." That brought down the house.

Lisa said, "Sam, you didn't even have a little clue?"

"No, I just knew you were behaving oddly. You were being too nice to me."

Oprah said, "Well, let's ask this the other way around. Lisa, when did you get interested in Sam?"

"I think after the second or third time he risked his life to get a story. I thought, 'Wouldn't it be great if he were risking his life for me?' Then I thought, 'Maybe he is!' And then I realized, 'He really is risking his life for me!' That's when I planned to propose to him after our dinner together."

"That was your first date, wasn't it? Even though you knew each other since high school?"

Lisa and Sam laughed. "It sure was," Sam said.

"I knew he'd never ask me out or ask me to marry him. So I did it."

"Lisa, so Sam was always shy?"

"Yes. He was a follower."

"And you had no interest in him in high school?"

"No, not romantically. I liked his steady work ethic and the quality of work he produced. I also liked the fact he didn't fight with me, like most everyone else did."

"Sam, would you say Lisa is hard to get along with?"

"Not for me." That also brought laughter.

"But what about other people?"

"They mostly got annoyed at Lisa because she criticized their work. And she doesn't sugarcoat things."

"So she just lets it all hang out when she gives her opinion?"

"I guess you could say that."

"Sam and Lisa, I'd like each of you to say what your scariest experience was during the whole adventure. You first, Sam."

"It was probably when Lisa was using the flamethrower around the presidential chopper and I was afraid it would blow up, killing him and us."

"I had it completely under control all the time!" Lisa protested.

"And how about you, Lisa? What scared you the most?"

"Probably when Sam drove the car headlong into the flock of turkeys on Navy Pier and we skidded our way through turkey guts. I was sure Sam would skid off into the lake."

"I had it completely under control all the time!" Sam said with a smile. More laughter from the audience. "But then right after that, when we were fighting the turkeys on Navy Pier and they burst through the window, I thought we were dead ducks."

"Yeah, I thought we were goners too," Lisa added.

"But the good old Chicago blizzard came through and froze them all," Oprah said. "So that Chicago cold and snow is good for something—freezing turkeys!

"Now that the crisis is all over and you're world famous, how has the whole experience affected you? Sam?"

"I've grown to really like the adventure of pursuing a story to its end. I was always persistent, but I had never had a story like this before."

"Lisa?"

"I was always worried about the bottom line. With a small-town newspaper, it is hard to make ends meet. I was always a pinchpenny, and I probably underpaid Sam."

"You did." He winked.

"But now that we've made it, money doesn't seem important at all. We've built up a good web presence, and that will continue to support our paper, but if we had to go back to just Sam and me, I'd be much happier and more relaxed than I was before. When you have love, money is less important." The audience applauded.

"Thank you so much, Sam and Lisa. We don't want you to go home empty handed. We've arranged with our sponsors from Buttery Turkeys for a lifetime supply of turkeys!" The audience laughed and cheered.

"And there is one more person who would like to personally thank you for helping him through this crisis: President Barack Obama!"

President Obama came onto stage with a big smile to thunderous applause. After shaking Sam's and Lisa's hands, he sat down. After the audience quieted, he said, "Sam and Lisa, you saved my life and, more importantly, the life of my wife and children. You were at the right place at the right time with the necessary help. Michelle and I would like to invite you to the White House—for a turkey dinner this New Year's!" The audience cheered wildly.

Sam said, "Lisa, did we have anything planned?"

"Well, there's the New Year's edition of the paper we have to get out. If we work overtime, we can have it ready by New Year's Eve. I think we could squeeze it in." The show closed in laughter.

* * *

Lashon's church provided a gospel choir for the wedding service, and her minister performed the ceremony. Rulon's groomsmen surprised everyone: they all wore beards, like Rulon, and they all had camo tuxes, like he did. Afterward, Rulon said he wanted a red-and-green effect for Christmas.

Lashon spent half her time yelling at him and half her time laughing.

Rulon got around surprisingly well on his new prosthetic legs. His stumps still got sore, so he sat quite a bit. At the reception, the cake had the little groom in camo, with a shotgun, and the bride with a flamethrower on her back. A zombie turkey, and a picture of the Shedd Aquarium on the cake, provided additional decorative touches.

The main meal consisted of a turkey buffet: roasted turkey, cold turkey slices on kaiser rolls, and turkey sausage and turkey bacon with eggs. The turkey sausage was *not* the Tuffield Genuine Zombie Turkey Sausage (not suitable for human consumption). The sausage came from turkeys Rulon had frozen long before the zombie plague. Lashon's "church ladies" had done the cooking and made the fixings.

"Where are you going for your honeymoon?" Lisa asked.

"We're going to Chicago," Lashon said.

"Chicago in the winter? You've got to be kidding."

"We want to see how it's doing after the zombie turkey plague. Also, Oprah has invited us on her show!"

"Say hi to her for us," Sam said.

"It's always been a dream of mine to be on her show," Rulon said.

"Me too," Lashon said. "Mom used to watch it all the time when I was growing up.

"After that, we're flying to Cancun. Rulon's making big money selling his turkey call on the *Midley Beacon* website."

Lisa smiled. The turkey calls sold for fifteen dollars each, and they were flying off the website by the thousands. The *Midley Beacon* made 10 percent profit on each one.

"Mind if we come along?" Sam asked.

"OK, but you can't share our honeymoon suite!" Rulon chimed in.

"I'd be happy to stay in a tent on the beach. You know we've never had a honeymoon."

"Now Sam, don't start. You know full well we've had two honeymoons at the *Midley Beacon*'s expense."

"The one we spent at a motel in Joliet and driving around Chicago trying to stay alive. The other we stayed in a motel in the middle of Nowhere, California, and spent the day walking through a field filled with rotting turkeys."

"It could have been worse."

"How?"

"They could have been live zombie turkeys."

* * *

Lashon and Rulon arrived at Oprah's studio for her show. She greeted them warmly and led them to the green room. When the time came, they went on stage in front of the audience.

"And here are the heroes of Shedd Aquarium and the Goodenow Nature Preserve, the newly married Mr. and Mrs. Rulon Miller!"

As they walked out, Lashon murmured to Rulon, "The set looks a lot smaller in person than it seems on TV."

"Let's get one thing out of the way first: you two just got married this weekend, right?'

"Yup, Saturday at Lashon's church in Gary," Rulon said.

"And you fell in love with each other right away, at the Shedd Aquarium?"

"Not right away," Lashon said hesitantly.

"Yes, right away. It was like coming back from the dead and waking up and seeing an angel."

Lashon laughed. "That was probably when it started—when he called me an angel."

"That's so romantic. Now, you're two very different people from different cultures—how is that working out for you?"

"I was a little nervous at first," Lashon said, "but Rulon gets along great with my family. And me with his family—they're all as friendly as he is."

"Our family's been on the south side of Chicago for many years," Rulon said. "We have many black friends and get along ducky."

"Does that mean you shoot your black friends?" Lashon joked.

"Only if they shoot first!" Rulon riposted.

Oprah laughed a little hesitantly at these non-politically-correct jokes. "The best news is there is no news. So now that all your adventures are over, what are your plans for the future?"

"First we're going to Cancun," Rulon said. The audience cheered.

"I didn't even give you that vacation," Oprah said.

"Then we're coming back to live on the south side of Chicago. Lashon will cover the Chicago area for the *Midley Beacon*, and I'll run my turkey-calling business."

"Can you blow your turkey call for us? I want the audience to imagine this echoing through Shedd Aquarium and the hundreds of zombie turkeys flocking to you." Oprah handed Rulon one of his turkey calls.

"I just got this from the *Midley Beacon* website this week." She smiled.

Rulon smiled back and said, "I always have one with me." He pulled one out of his camo hunting outfit.

GOBBLE! GOBBLE!

Oprah jumped.

"I jumped too when I first heard that," Lashon commented.

"This is the genuine All Turkey Call. The best of the best, it calls hens, toms, and zombies."

"I hope we don't get any zombie turkeys in here!" Oprah said half joking, half nervous.

Rulon smiled broadly and said, "You never can tell when they'll pop up!" He then pulled his bowie knife out of his pants leg. "But I'm ready for them!"

"Lashon, doesn't it make you nervous when Rulon carries around that pig-sticker, or should I say, turkey sticker?"

"Not at all!" Lashon reached into her ample bosom and pulled out her bowie knife. "I've gotten pretty good at carving turkeys with this thing. This was Rulon's first gift to me. See the inscription? As Rulon says, 'Don't leave home without it!'"

"This seems like a good point to show our audience some of the most famous zombie turkey battles." Oprah then played some footage from the zombie turkey attacks at the Shedd Aquarium and Goodenow Nature preserve.

"Yup, that's when I used this baby at Goodenow. It kept me alive for over an hour," Lashon said.

"That's amazing. And as a good-bye gift to all the audience members from the Millers, under each chair, is a zombie turkey call!" The audience erupted in applause and laughter.

"And for the Millers, Lashon and Rulon, we have arranged to pay for their trip to Cancun, their hotel, and all their meals!" The audience cheered wildly. "And that's not all. They'll also be driving their new 2016 Cadillac Escalade!"

Rulon and Lashon were struck mute by Oprah's largesse. "I figured Rulon would like the four-wheel drive and Lashon would like the comfortable luxury."

"You got that right!" Lashon said.

"I still like my truck—but I don't mind this!" Rulon said.

* * *

On New Year's Eve, Hank Williams took Betty Tuffield out to dinner to Clucks, a local restaurant in Henry, famed for its fried chicken.

"I've got a business proposal for you, Betty."

"I'm all ears," she said with a smile, holding a cob of corn in her hands.

"How would you like to run my turkey business? I know you were successful running Tom's, and that would take a big burden from me, handling all that accounting and marketing. I could then focus on breeding turkeys and expand my flock."

"That's a good idea, but my plate is already pretty full between my sausage business and ZoTWHA." Her eyes narrowed suspiciously. "You already knew that. What's up? What's the other shoe to drop?"

"This." He knelt to the floor. "Betty Tuffield, will you marry me?"

"Oh!" Then she laughed. "Listen to me. I sound like a flustered teenage girl! But I am flustered and surprised. Hank Williams, I will be glad to be your wife! I hoped for this, but never dreamt it would come so soon!"

They kissed and then planned the merger of their businesses and Betty's exit from ZoTWHA.

* * *

On New Year's Eve, Sam and Lisa flew first class to Washington, DC, at the government's expense, to dine with the president and his family. The presidential limousine met them at the Ronald Reagan Washington National Airport and motored them to the White House. There they visited with the president, Michelle, Sasha, and Malia.

"Hi, Sam, Lisa," President Obama greeted them.

"Mr. President, it's an honor to be here," Lisa said.

"The pleasure is all mine," the president said. "It's the least I could do after you saved my life and my family's."

Sam and Lisa also greeted the Secret Service agents they recognized from the car ride in downtown Chicago.

They all sat down to a turkey dinner. Chef Philippe came out and said, "This seemed appropriate, considering how the last dinner went. This is my make up for the Thanksgiving dinner you all missed. I have gotten a zombie test kit from the Turkey Institute, and these turkeys have all tested clean."

"Now that you mention it," Sam remarked, "we never did have a Thanksgiving turkey. We were working on Thanksgiving."

"How well I know," the president said. "And I'm glad you were."

"I've got to say," Michelle Obama said, "at first I thought the scariest part of that day was when the zombie turkeys attacked us in the house. Then when the helicopter crashed, I thought that was the worst, but the worst of all was, after all that, when I saw that L train bearing down on us."

"S'funny thing. Oprah asked us the same thing. I thought it was when the flames roared up to the helicopter. Lisa thought it was when we almost skidded off Navy Pier. But we both agree—when the window broke and the turkeys came pouring in at Navy Pier, we thought we were goners," Sam said.

"Sasha, Malia, what scared you the most that day?" Lisa asked.

"It was when the helicopter crashed—" Sasha began

"No, it was when the train was coming—" Malia interrupted.

"And then we had to climb down those Secret Service agents," Malia finished.

"How are they doing? I heard one lost his eye."

"Agent Smith's recuperating well," the president said. "We've given him recognition and offered him full retirement, but he still wants to work in the Secret Service."

For dessert they had the traditional pumpkin pie with whipped cream, and pecan pie. For entertainment, they watched Alfred Hitchcock's *The Birds* in the White House movie theater. The president chuckled. "It seems appropriate after all we've been through."

Sasha and Malia hadn't seen the movie before. The others hadn't seen it for a long time. It seemed a little tame, but parts of it resonated with their experiences. Sasha and Malia were pleasantly surprised that such an old movie could be so good.

After that, they all watched the New Year come in on the television. They watched it roll in Sydney, Tokyo, Cairo, Berlin, Paris, London, Rio de Janeiro, and then New York City.

The president proposed a toast. "Here's to a happy, turkey-free New Year!"

"Hear, hear!" Sam said. "Or maybe I should say, 'Gobble, gobble!'" They all laughed and drank champagne.

Epilogue

"Hey, Will, we had some reporters here the other day," Mark Victor commented to his friend and fellow truck driver Will Ahern at the bar after work one day.

"So what?"

"They were asking about what we did with the grain from Corn-All."

"Oho! What did you tell them?"

"The usual—that we dumped it in the landfill."

"They didn't ask to see the grain?"

"Nope. They did ask how long it would be exposed."

"Not for long, I know. They didn't go digging in the landfill looking for it, did they?"

"Nah. They did ask if there were animals around the landfill."

"Whatcha say?"

"I never saw any."

"Neither did I. It looks like they didn't catch on to our scam."

"I don't think they had a clue we were selling that grain at your brother's grain silo."

"And then he sold it back to Corn-All!" Will chuckled.

"And then we charged people to load our trucks with their fill and took it back to the Corn-All dump."

"And at such low prices!" Will laughed.

"How can we stay in business?" Mark laughed with him.

After their laughter died down, Mark took a sip of his beer and said more seriously, "You know, I think they were actually working another angle than our scam."

"What do ya mean?"

"I have no clue. That's why I'm a little worried."
"Forget about it. It'll come to nothing."

* * *

He felt great, full of energy. He ate a nut from his stores. He went down his tree and out to breed with some females. He saw a really good one with a sexy, bushy tail. As he chased her toward her tree, a hawk swooped down and killed him. The hawk never noticed the squirrel's red eyes.

* * *

He felt great, full of energy. He bred with all his does. When he was done, he went out of his warren, looking for more does. He automatically avoided going into the open, avoiding hawks instinctively, but he knew where the next warren was. He defeated the buck with his superior strength and bred with his does. And on to the next warren. He did not look back, but all the rabbits in both warrens were red eyed.

* * *

He felt great, full of energy. He looked at the fence separating him from the cows. He had avoided it in the past because it burned his hide when he touched it, but now he didn't care. He charged it, burst the wires, and sped to the cows. After breeding with them all, he looked around for more. He found them in the next field. He burst through that fence. There was a bull there, but he quickly overpowered it. That bull didn't have red eyes like he did.

* * *

Donald Newby had been a computer programmer for three years, ever since he got out of college. He'd been paying off his student loans by living in his parents' basement. That gave him plenty of time for online gaming: DOTA (Defense of the Ancients) was his favorite. Occasionally, he wanted to go out with girls, but he couldn't figure out how to find one, let alone how to start a conversation with one. He'd read about people meeting in nightclubs and bars, but that didn't make sense; he didn't dance or drink.

He vaguely realized he wasn't a girl's ideal man: below average height and overweight. He figured he'd just find some girl who wasn't ideal. Any girl would do, when you had none.

Tonight was a big night for him. He was going to the DOTA convention, where he'd meet his fellow players, discuss strategy, and play DOTA. He had a faint hope he'd meet some girls. There were rumored to be some girl gamers, and some players claimed to be girls online, but he was skeptical. People could say anything on the net.

He had chili and cornbread, his favorite, for supper, with his mom and dad. Dad was an accountant. Mom volunteered at church. Idly, he read the ingredients on the Corn-All cornbread mix box. Corn meal. He wondered if they used GMO modified corn? He wasn't really concerned; there didn't seem to be any danger to it.

He checked his DOTA T-shirt in the mirror before he left. It looked good, in black, green, and red. He made sure it was not tucked in—that way he'd hide his stomach. He just looked like a big square guy. Sort of like SpongeBob SquarePants.

As he drove downtown to the convention after supper, he was getting more and more excited and keyed up. Maybe there actually were girls who played computer games! Maybe they would like him! Maybe—he hardly could think this to himself—maybe they'd have sex with him!

He got into the convention center and was stunned. There were dozens, even hundreds of girls there! He picked one, probably too good looking for him, and started talking to her about DOTA. He didn't recognize her screen name "Angel of Death," but she recognized his: "Zombie Mage." They discussed various players and teams they knew. Her name was Maggie Unsicher. She was dark haired, short, and plump.

"My name is Don Newby," he told her.

She was really knowledgeable about DOTA and other computer games. They spent the whole convention together, playing on teams, eating junk food, discussing strategy.

He didn't know how to ask her for sex. "Do you want to go out someplace afterward?" he asked in a rush.

"Sure." She smiled at him. He melted.

They went to his car in the parking lot. A mugger jumped them. He held a knife.

"Gimmie your money!"

"OK," Maggie said, handing him her purse.

"You too, wimp," he growled at Donald.

All the excitement that had been building all evening came to a climax. He had never felt better, stronger, faster. He felt brave. He grabbed his wallet and threw it in the mugger's face. Then he hit him as hard as he could on the side of his head. The mugger fell like he'd been hit with a sledgehammer.

Don looked at his fist. That hadn't hurt at all. It was easy! He was sorry there weren't more bad guys to punch out. It was just like being a video game hero!

"You were wonderful!" Maggie said and hugged him.

Don had never been hugged by a girl before. It was beyond all his expectations.

"I'd do anything for you, Maggie! Where do you want to go?"

"A motel," she said.

And off they went. Maggie never noticed Donald's red eyes, because hers were red too.

The End of *Zombie Turkeys*

and the beginning of zombie USA.

My Undead Mother in Law

Chapter 1 - Gary

"You know I love your mother. But your mother's a zombie. Who wants to see one zombie, let alone four of them?"

"Now that's not fair. Mom and Dad have adjusted to their zombiism very well. Mom still volunteers at church and bakes cookies and pies for the bake sales. Dad still works as an accountant at GM. There's nothing to worry about!"

"That covers Diane and George. I know them. I guess I'm ready for them. What about your brother and this new girlfriend of his? I don't think Don has said two whole sentences to me since I've known him!"

"He'd never get a word in edgewise, with you Ron. You said it yourself; you've had diarrhea of the mouth since you were born. He and his friend Maggie will be fine."

"Whatever you say, Karen," I knew when to surrender. I focused my eyes on the Indiana turnpike ahead.

"Hmmph!"

I glanced at Karen while I drove. Her arms were crossed under her breasts and she looked out the window, away from me. Trying to make peace, I said, "I thought we dodged a bullet when the zombie turkey plague just missed Gary

Indiana. I never dreamt this zombie thing would hit our own family." I said in a carefully neutral tone.

"So far, it hasn't hit us hard. Life goes on as usual."

Great! At least she's talking to me. "As great as it can with glowing red eyes," I said with a big grin.

"I suppose. I hadn't really thought about how hard life would be, like that."

"I have no clue what that'd be like."

"Clueless from Toledo!"

"Clueless going to Gary." We laughed. "Remember our rehearsal dinner?" I said.

"Sure. That was six years ago. Hard to believe."

"Your Mom and I got along fine there. We dominated the conversation, as I recall. I hardly noticed the rest of your family. I do remember your Dad impressing me with his analytical mind. Did Don even talk? He's like a mute bivalve."

"Yes, a little, to me."

"Well, I don't remember anything.' I only had eyes for you'," I warbled.

"Ha! Good thing I didn't hear you sing before I said 'I do'."

"I'm sure you did."

"I'm sure I wouldn't notice. I was too amazed I got to marry the 'Big Man on Campus', college graduate and internet marketer, Ron Yardley."

"So why did a beautiful girl like you marry a guy like me?"

"I still don't think I'm beautiful, just average. You're the good looking one!"

"Thank you, but you're wrong. You're the good looking one. I'm just average."

"We'll have to agree to disagree."

We settled into a companionable silence for ten miles or so. Then I said, "I know why I'm so reluctant to meet your family."

"Why?"

"I did some marketing for the *Midley Beacon* during the turkey apocalypse last Thanksgiving and then later for author Andy Zach's book about it, *Zombie Turkeys*. I saw a lot of bloody photos and videos and read too many gory details. I never liked the idea of pretend zombies, let alone real life ones. I was just glad we missed it in Toledo. Now I'm in the middle of it."

"Now Ron, meeting my family, even if they're zombies, doesn't put you in the middle of another zombie apocalypse."

"Yeah, you're right." That was the ultimate solution to any marital disagreement, I've found.

"What's Don's girlfriend's name again?"

"Maggie. Maggie Unsicker. Mom said they were going to announce their engagement this weekend, for Valentine's Day. That's why we're going. Remember?"

"Of course. I wonder why so few people have turned zombie? First, there were zombie squirrels, then zombie rabbits, then zombie cows, and finally, a dozen people or so turned zombie."

"None of those zombies were really numerous like the turkeys were."

"Thank God for that! What does Maggie do, anyway? Besides play video games like Don, I mean."

"Maggie's a phlebotomist and a lab technician at Methodist Hospital in Gary."

"A what?"

"Phlebotomist. She takes blood samples from people and then runs lab tests on them."

As we pull up in their drive, I'm reassured by the sheer normality of their three-bedroom suburban home: Green yard, partially covered with snow, evergreen bushes, two car garage. There is no sign zombies live there. Of course, what sign could I expect? A skull and crossbones and 'Beware of Zombies'? Perhaps a biohazard sign?

Diane greets us at the door. "Hello, my love!" She hugged Karen. Karen barely flinched as she looked into her mother's bright, red eyes. But she grunted "Ugh!" at the force of her embrace.

"Ease up Mom."

"Oh, sorry."

"Hello Mom," I said, as I hugged her as hard I as could. She hugged me back twice as hard. "Ugh," I grunted too. Diane still had blonde-highlighted brown hair, as she did when I first met her. She'd gained a pound or two, though. She smelled of the body talc "White Linen". I recognized it because Karen and I bought it for her birthday last year, pre-zombie. And she still wore her cat's eye reading glasses on a chain around her neck.

Diane seated us on the living room sofa. "Suppers on. I have a nice pot roast for us tonight. Donnie and Maggie should be here soon. George!" She called. "The kids are here!"

A heavy tread down the stairs announced George Newby. His eyes shone red too, but while Diane was built like a middle-aged woman, George was a classic wide-body. His shoulders filled the stairway. You'd think he was a truck driver or a lineman, rather than an accountant.

"Hi, Karen. Hi, Ron." he rumbled. He hugged his daughter, like he held a baby bird, and shook my hand without hurting me in his bratwurst fingers.His bright red eyes looked squarely into mine.

"I'm so glad you made the trip. You can help us put to rest the ugly rumors that people with zombiism aren't human. It's just a disease. It's not even harmful," enthused Diane.

"Mom, we love you. You don't have to convince us." I said.

"Of course not. I know that. It's just that we've had people talking behind our backs at church and the public health officials trying to pressure us to get the treatment to eliminate the disease."

"Don't you want to get rid of it? I think the antibiotics for it are safe and effective."

"You'd think so, but we actually have never felt better in our lives! I have more energy than ever, and so does George-- right George?"

"Yup."

"My arthritic aches and pains have completely disappeared and George's old football knee injury is all better too."

Looking out the window, George said, "Don and Maggie just pulled up."

Entering the room, Don looked like a smaller version of his Dad, with the same squat build. Maggie was also short and plump and attractive in a round sort of way.

I'm glad Karen got all the good-looking genes in the family, I thought to myself.

We sat down to dinner. The pot roast was delicious. Diane made it with caramelized onions and mushrooms, mixed with carrots and potatoes. Seeing four pairs of shining red eyes around the table twisted my stomach around the pot roast. I wrestled my stomach into submission and tried not to think about it.

For dessert, we had a New York style cheesecake, decorated with a big heart and "Be My Valentine" on the top. It was good but didn't make me feel any better about the zombie apocalypse dinner.

"We have the two old sweethearts, me and George, the recent sweethearts, Karen and Ron, and the new sweethearts, Don and Maggie!" Diane announced enthusiastically. She divided the cake into six equal sections.

"Oh, that's too much for me!" Karen exclaimed.

"OK, how about half?"

"That's fine."

Everyone else ate the big portion of cake. Diane noticed me watch her eat hers and commented, "Our appetite has really picked up recently. We're eating more, but not gaining weight."

"That alone gives us reason to stay zombie," Don spoke for the first time. Becoming a powerful zombie really brought Don out of his shell. I didn't expect him to speak at all.

"Yes, we were talking about people pressuring us to get treatment before you came."

"Over my dead body!" Don said fiercely and then laughed at the irony.

"That'd actually be pretty hard to do," Maggie said with a smile. Zombie jokes arose spontaneously around the Newby's dinner table.

"And now, you two, don't you have an announcement?" Diane looked at them expectantly.

Maggie looked at Don, raising her eyebrows in question. Or maybe, she meant, 'She's your mother.' "What did you have in mind, Mom?" Don asked with a frown.

"Didn't you say you'd get engaged this weekend?"

"Yeah, we talked about it, but we don't see the point. We're happy living together."

"You *told* me you'd propose to Maggie this weekend!" Diane's outrage crept into her voice.

"Yeah, but I changed my mind."

"You *promised!*" Diane stood and yelled, "Don't lie to your mother!"

"We're adults," Don stood too. "We're allowed to change our minds. And don't yell at me like a little kid." Don stood too, glaring. at his mother.

"You're adults, but you can't live in adultery. If you ever want to stay in our house, you *have* to get married!"

"We don't *have* to do anything! Let's go, Maggie." Don reached to take Maggie's hand, but Diane rushed to him and grabbed his other hand.

"No, you don't! You won't leave until we settle this and you agree to get married!"

"Don't be silly Mom. You can't stop me." He tried to push her away, but she clung burrlike to his arm.

"Don't make me angry!" she threatened.

Finally, with a convulsive fling, he pushed her across the room. The wallboard dented where she hit. Don looked startled by his own action.

George suddenly stood up, like a mountain rising from the sea. The chair shot out behind him, hitting another section of the dining room and cracking it.

"Don—" he began, firm as a stone.

"So you want to be rough, do you?" Diane's sudden soft tone was far more chilling than her yelling. Every eye, red and otherwise, focused on her. Diane's eyes narrowed. George stopped, waiting.

My Undead Mother-in-law will be available for sale on Amazon in July 2017. Check my blog, zombieturkeys.com for the latest news.

Andy Zach

Author Bio

Photo by Barb Lloyd

Andy Zach was born Anastasius Zacharias, in Greece. His parents were both zombies. Growing up, he loved animals of all kinds. After moving to the United States as a child, in high school he won a science fair by bringing toads back from suspended animation. Before turning to fiction, Andy published his PhD thesis "Methods of Revivification for Various Species of the Kingdom Animalia" in the prestigious JAPM, *Journal of Paranormal Medicine*. Andy, in addition to being the foremost expert on paranormal animals, enjoys breeding phoenixes. He lives in Illinois with his five phoenixes.

QUICK ORDER FORM

Satisfaction Guaranteed

⌨ **Web site orders:** zombieturkeys.com
⌨ jms61614-andyzach@yahoo.com
🖅 **Postal orders:**   Zombie Turkey Orders
                          PO Box 10705
                          Peoria, Illinois 61614

Please send the following Books

I understand that I may return any of them for a full refund—for any reason, no questions asked.
See our website for FREE information on:
Contests, giveaways, other books, speaking/interviews, mailing lists, fan discussion forums

Name:

Address:

City, State/Province, Postal Code

Tel:

Email:

Sales tax:

Shipping by air:

Payment: Cheque; credit card: Visa, MasterCard, Optima, AMEX, Discover
Card number:
Name on card: Exp. date: /

Made in the USA
Monee, IL
18 November 2021

82466451R00105